Interlude

Olivia Sanner

Contents

Chapter 1

D ev Malhotra stood at the far edge sixty-three floors above the earth.

Dressed in a crisp black suit, his long frame was leaned over a solid glass balustrade. He sipped from a glass of whiskey, letting the warm liquid prickle his throat. The evening should've made him feel elated, instead he found himself somber and forlorn. His gaze was narrowed at the jaw-dropping sight of the city that lay below him.

Vancouver was beautiful, most would agree. But from the sixty third floor of a Downtown high-rise, it was breathtaking. A lively city with long roads, tall structures reaching for the skies and thick clusters of trees sprinkled with remnants of February snow, all traveling towards the white peaks of the gigantic mountain range far ahead. At present, dark clouds with low, ambient moonlight were closer than ever before. If someone tip-toed and stretched one hand, a little bit higher, they were sure to graze a star or two.

Behind him, the open rooftop was bustling with high energy. Servers shuffled with stacks of plates and glasses, and assistants spoke furiously into headsets. At a random moment, all at once, the area was lit with innumerable yellow bulbs running along invisible lines, suspended high above.

But today Dev noticed neither the extravagance of the city nor the splendor of the party that was about to commence. Early in the morning, he had stayed in bed for a long time, staring at the calendar on his iPad. A long past memory had resurfaced like a yearly reminder.

The memory of a beautiful girl with light brown hair and sky blue eyes.

It was hard to tell whether it became less or more painful with each passing year.

As the guests began to pour in, he made himself focus on them.

"Good to see you, Dev." Gerry Chen shook his hand. "Where's Ranjeet?"

"Dad's flight was delayed. He should be here soon." Dev signaled to a server who appeared with a tray of drinks. "Campbell Estate is turning out well, I hear. I would love to get a tour."

"Anytime! Anytime for you, my boy." Gerry clapped one hand on the younger man's shoulder and smiled fondly. "Now, tell me more about the Gallo house you're doing up in Whistler."

Morningstar Properties, a massive real estate company, was owned and operated by the four Malhotra brothers. The new generation of Malhotra heirs and heiress, with their sophisticated degrees and influential network of peers, had elevated Morningstar Properties into a renowned real estate enterprise. The Malhotra family itself resonated with wealth, fortune and fame.

As a strategic plan from a marketing and branding perspective, they threw lavish parties from time to time. In the beginning only people from real estate longed to be invited. But slowly as the family fortune and network grew, celebrities and socialites made frequent appearances.

The open terrace was now crowded with prominent, well-dressed women and men. Drinks were poured, fancy appetizers flowed in abundance and an upbeat music filled the air. The decor had been deliberately arranged to eliminate a focal point. Outdoor sofas and chairs were set up in a clever and cyclic harmony along the large terrace. But this effort was made redundant by a single man.

Dev Malhotra, the heir to the Malhotra family and Morningstar Properties, had a natural flair for inadvertently turning himself into a focal point. Not just when he spoke but even while listening, he held people around with some invisible, gentle force that they felt compelled to adhere to.

He circled through the party with an expert ease, charming his guests. He was intelligent and highly perceptive. Not only because he studied engineering and went to business school, but because he had a genuine desire for knowledge. And because he went to great lengths to seek it. His opinions were hardly ever vague or given thoughtlessly. He was an expert in his field and whatever didn't fall into his sphere, he knew where to look, which people to hire and whom to seek advice from. At twenty-six, he was presumably one of the most sought-after bachelors in his social sphere.

"Congratulations, Dev. Edgewater Homes is sold out. And in record time." Helena Nielson, the CEO of Streetside Investments raised a glass to his recently completed project of town-homes in Abbotsford.

Dev smiled, raising his own glass in response.

He presented an impressive stature, six feet tall with a lean athletic built, broad shoulders and muscular arms. He had a handsome face; sharp, angular features and a solid cut jaw. Thick black hair framed a set of luminous eyes, the color of the earth, which glowed vibrantly against the natural tan of his skin. A dark stubble added shades of fearless vigor to his portrait of boyishness. He smiled easily and often, mesmerizing his audience without meaning to.

It was easy - very, very easy - for young women to sigh and pine at the sight of him. On rare occasions, he was seen with beautiful dates but as far as the female population in their society was concerned, Dev Malhotra was very much in the game.

"And the Willowbark Estate? Was that yours as well?" asked Jeremy Carter, a veteran architect in his fifties, visiting from California. "It was small but very well done."

"It was. But that was built by Nathan Napier."

The world of North American real estate was a giant web of delicately formed connections. A lot of the action happened behind the scenes, often by people who chose discretion over fame. Not just anyone had the privilege to be privy to every piece of information. Dev, however, belonged to the group who lived in the center of this extravagant chaos.

"Nathan Napier is doing homes in Canada now?" Carter said with a note of disapproval. "UK run out of land?"

"Canadian real estate is burning off the charts as we speak. Would you blame anyone for dipping their hands into it?" Dev chuckled.

"I suppose not. Last I heard, Napier was using one of his lackeys for his recent homes."

His eyes twinkled with amusement. "I know for a fact that this time, the particular lackey happens to be a very accomplished architect."

Carter's eyebrows rose with intrigue. "You've met him?"

Dev grinned. "He's here."

"Really?" Carter asked, though not the least bit surprised that Dev had already managed to fraternize with the newest architect in business. "I must meet this lackey then. Where is he?"

"I'd like to meet him too." Helena added with eagerness.

"He should have arrived by now." Dev scanned the party. He was about pull his phone and make a call when something caught his attention.

You have got to be joking! Dev groaned under his breath.

"Something wrong?" Helena inquired.

"Not at all. Excuse me."

On the farthest corner, where the lights glowed the dimmest and the din of the conversations reached the slowest, the said lackey was casually hiding. His tall, lean body was reclined comfortably on a chaise, fingers typing on his phone with a single-minded focus; the fanfare around nonexistent to him.

Dev took a seat on a chair opposite to the man. Looking skyward momentarily, he prayed for patience. The man continued typing.

"It's Saturday, Nash." Dev stated plainly.

For a moment, Avinash Singh turned from his phone then he went back to typing. There was a pause when his mind finally registered Dev's presence. He blinked, a little dazed, straightened himself and slipped his phone back inside the pocket of his suit jacket.

"You cannot be working right now." Dev gave his old college mate an incredulous look.

"How's the party going?" Nash asked, eager to shift focus.

Dev shook his head, his face breaking into a slow smile. It was hard to get upset at Nash. The man was dedicated to his work with the naivety and discipline of a saint. That he was actually present here in the first place was a testament to their friendship.

"Why don't you go around and talk?" Dev encouraged.

"Yeah, later." Nash waved one hand in dismissal. "Isn't Roman coming?"

"No, he texted earlier. Still stuck in London."

Nash picked up his drink from the side table and pulled a long gulp. His eyes drifted over Dev's shoulder. "Oh, there's Matt Sherman"

"Who?" Dev asked.

"The interior designer I used for Willowbark. I invited him. Hope you don't mind. The guy's talented and eagerly looking for work."

Dev glanced over his shoulder. "Of course. I'd like to meet him mys—"

He froze.

Matt Sherman had stepped inside to reveal a young woman dressed in a short black dress.

The noise around Dev was squashed. It was as if someone had abruptly switched off a very loud radio. His guests, Nash, they had all seized to exist. The winds picked up an unreal momentum and it seemed like at least half the lights had burst. His gaze was transfixed on the girl - unblinking, unwavering and severe in disbelief. She was making her way through the crowd, getting close in his general direction. Matt had waved to Nash and the latter said something, but Dev wasn't listening. He was aware of nothing. Every shred of cognizance had left his body save for one - he noticed that she had suddenly bolted to a halt; the same glaring recognition on her face. He couldn't look away, not even for a second. He was drinking in the sight of her.

The sight he hadn't seen in eight years.

The sight of a girl in light brown hair and sky blue eyes.

The sight of...his Rose.

Chapter 2

Dev didn't know what happened in the next moment but something had changed. Rose had gasped in shock, one hand snapped to her chest. It was only when Nash was at his side, did Dev become aware of a sharp pain emerging from his palm which was now smeared with blood.

He had smashed the glass in his hand to pieces.

"Dev!" Nash cried, snatching napkins from a table. "You're bleeding, mate."

"You knew she was coming?" Dev asked, his voice barely above a whisper.

Nash looked flabbergasted. "No. That's just Matt's assistant. What's wrong?"

"That's her." He whispered, eyes affixed on the brown haired girl.

Nash didn't understand right away. But when he did, his eyes grew wide with shock and recognition. He glanced at Rose then back at Dev. Finding his sense of composure, he caught a passing server and whispered some instruction.

Rose was still standing like a statue, staring open mouthed. All feeling and every thought had abandoned her. She wanted to turn around and run but her limbs were no longer in her control, suspended purely by his piercing gaze.

She wouldn't move unless he allowed her to.

A moment later the event manager, Lea, appeared looking worried that something had gone wrong with her decor. She took in their odd stance, then her eyes flew to Dev's bloodied hand.

"What happened?" Lea exclaimed.

"A small accident." Nash replied, his voice calm and controlled. "Is there some place we can get a little privacy?"

She pointed to a far corner behind to the left. "There's a back room."

"Good. Get some first aid supplies. If anyone asks, tell them Dev got a call."

Lea nodded frantically, scrambling away.

Dev blinked, his gaze finally leNashng her.

It was like a switch. A wave of consciousness returned. Rose jerked and took a step to the side. But before she could run, a deep, masculine voice pronounced a single word.

"Stop." Dev commanded. It was spoken without emphasis or amplification but it rang in her ears and rushed all the way to her toes.

She froze. She didn't want to stop; she had to. It was pure instinct to yield to the sound of his voice...a compulsive, unconscious response that she had been born with. The loud chaos of the world never mattered; his voice had always filtered through, encroaching into the depths her mind.

He took one step toward her, then another. A tight coil clenched in her chest, making it hard for her to breathe. He'd always been tall. But now, years later, with his imposing form and the rage in his eyes, he towered over her.

Dev dipped his head lower. A familiar scent transported him to a giant oak tree below a sunlight sky. He inched closer. The warmth of his breath made her to shiver. His lips parted and he whispered something into her ear. Only a few words. But her eyes grew wide with bewilderment. She nearly whimpered. No longer able to withstand it, she turned and bolted.

Lea appeared, nudging Dev toward the back room. He stood stoic for a moment then gave Nash a meaningful look. With a silent nod, he turned on his heel and let Lea usher him away.

Rose was past the exit and headed towards the main elevator by the time Nash caught up to her.

"Rose, wait —"

But before he could say anything further, she turned to him and muttered insensibly, "Thank you for inviting me, I mean, Matt."

Nash shook his head. "That's not important. Are you alright?"

"This was a bad idea." Her face was pale and forehead creased with worry. "I shouldn't have come without knowing the host. Matt said it was an important event so I just tagged along. I didn't know..." she continued miserably, staring at the jagged carpet underneath their feet. "I didn't know he was..." Her head snapped up to face him. She blurted with emotion, "I didn't know!"

"It's alright." Nash tried to move closer. When she backed up, he realized that she was too disoriented so he took a step back. "You're in the same city now, in the same line of work. You would've met sooner or later."

"Later would've been nice."

"Look, I won't ask you to stay," Nash sighed, "because I know you won't. I just want to make sure you can get home safely."

"Of course, I can."

He was unconvinced. "Give me your phone." he stretched out one palm, "I'll put my number in. When you get home, I want you to send me a message."

"I really can take care of myself, you know." she bit between her teeth.

"Humor me."

To his surprise and relief, she complied.

"You know then?" she accused, suddenly, taking him off guard. "Our story?"

Nash exhaled a heavy breath, handing her phone back. "I know what Dev told me." He felt bad for her. She was a nice girl, genuinely talented and dedicated to her job. They had spoken directly only a couple of times but he'd seen her in the background, working diligently with Matt.

"I've admired your work." she said, bitterly. "And I'd hope I would get to work with you in the future. But I suppose you hate me too."

"No." He replied, firm and low. "This has no effect on our professional side."

When the elevator sprung open, she leapt inside. Just before the doors closed, Nash spoke, his eyes serious and careful, "He doesn't hate you."

An hour later, when Rose stepped into her apartment, the full force of emotion came rushing back. The sound of her cries filled her lonely bedroom. Her gaze landed on the suitcase at the bottom corner of her small closet. She tried to look away, tried to stop herself, but ultimately couldn't. Her body thrust forward, sinking to the floor; trembling fingers yanked the heavy suitcase. Under the meticulously packed items, lay a faded yellow envelope. Every picture from their youth had been deleted from her computer, phone, online accounts, external hard drives - everywhere. Frames had been smashed and gifts had been thrown away. Anger and hurt had destroyed all their memories.

Save for this.

Gently, she undid the clasp and lifted the flap. A small sea shell stumbled out, barely fitting in the quarter of her palm. It was dark beige with prominent streaks of muddy brown.

"Seriously? This is what you found?" a younger male voice echoed in her ear.

"It's perfect. I'm keeping it." she'd said, quite pleased with herself.

The memory had been locked away in a distant corner of her heart.

She slid her hand into the envelope and pulled out an old photograph. It was the only one left; the sole physical proof that their story had been real. She blinked with effort, clearing the silent tears that continued to pour, hot against her cheek. An image flashed before her eyes - his bloodied hand, his daunting form and the rage that blazed in those earthy brown eyes.

The photograph in her hand, however, played a different scene altogether.

Against the backdrop of a festive carnival, was a stolen moment frozen in time: An eighteen-year-old boy stood behind an eighteen-year-old girl, one arm looped around her waist and rested on her stomach. She in turn, had entwined her fingers with his. He was a bit scrawny and she had braces. But their smiles were brighter than the glaring lights behind.

She was running fast, almost sure that she would win this time. In a few long strides, his arms wrapped around her waist bringing them to a halt.

"I win!" he whispered, breathlessly, taking in the scent of her hair.

The warmth from his chest enveloped her, as the rapid beat of his heart thumped against her back. Her laughter ran far through the lush green fields. "I'm going to run faster tomorrow." she challenged. "And even faster the day after. You won't be able to catch me then."

"I'll still catch you." The finality of his words betrayed his naive age. "Always."

Once upon a time, Rose and Dev had lived in an innocent story, unaware that the world beyond their oak tree would tear them apart.

She lay in bed all night staring out the open window. Sleep wouldn't come to her aid. Not tonight. Her mind replayed the moment from the party, when he'd leaned in to whisper into her ear. He'd smelled of whiskey, rich perfume and something so familiar that it terrified her. In a harsh, low baritone he had said three words -

"Happy Birthday, Rose."

Chapter 3

"How long are you able to stay?" Dev asked, reaching for the bottle from the side table.

"Two weeks." Nash replied.

"And then?"

"Tuscany."

Dev gave him a look.

"Nathan has a commission in the country side. I want to see how it's going."

"By commission you mean?"

Nash averted his gaze. "It's a villa."

"For?"

Nash picked his bottle of beer and took a gulp. Turning to his friend, he winked.

Dev shook his head. "Of course. You can't talk about your top secret clients."

"They aren't my clients. They're Nathan's clients."

"Sure." Dev smirked. "Who is it this time? Movie star? Sportsperson? Or plain old Royalty?"

"I'm not sure if this one actually has a title."

Nash had replied with genuine thought; it made Dev chuckle.

"What?" Nash gave his friend a strange look.

"And you're still working for free?"

"Well," he held the neck of the bottle between two fingers, idling swinging it. "Not free, exactly. He covers all my expenses. I never use my own card."

"But he doesn't pay you."

Nash shrugged, unbothered by this. His work involved a lot of travel and for the most part, his home moved from one hotel room to another. Whenever he came to Vancouver, he stayed with Dev or Roman (or both) and made it a point to spends a few extra days with his old college mate. This time, Nash had arrived two days prior, just hours before Dev's party. The boys had been so busy with their work that it was only now that they could take a break.

"There is something I want to talk to you about." Nash began cautiously.

Dev glanced at him, waiting.

"I don't want you to go theatrical on me." Nash said, warily.

"Theatrical?" Dev narrowed his eyes.

Nash sighed, combing one hand through his dark hair. He was really not looking forward to the conversation. Still, it had to be done.

"What's wrong?" Dev asked, concerned.

Having little skill to ease into a sensitive topic, Nash blurted, "Rose needs help." Then added to clarify. "Er, a job."

The instantaneous change on Dev's face was exactly the look that Nash had been dreading. Dev's jaw tensed. His eyes stilled. "How do you know this?"

"Matt Sherman told me."

"When?"

"This afternoon."

Dev nodded as if approving his friend's prompt decision to have a direct conversation. Had Nash withheld the information, Dev's anger wouldn't have been easily placated.

"What did Sherman say?" Dev demanded in a low voice.

"He asked if I know anyone hiring a junior interior designer." Nash explained. "Sherman's own design assistant is returning from her break so he doesn't have room for another one. Apparently, he'd told Rose in the beginning that the position he offered was only for three months. But at the time she'd been desperate for a job. He thinks she was hoping something else would've worked out in the meantime. But it hasn't. So she needs a suitable job and," Nash muttered the next words with utmost reluctance. "And money." He took a heavy breath and continued. "Sherman doesn't want her to go but he doesn't have the resources to take on another assistant. Still, he hates to see her being wasted at some random position. He believes she has a real talent."

Yes, she does. Dev thought, ruefully. "When does her work end with Sherman?"

"End of next week."

Dev's lips were pressed into a tight line. He set the bottle aside and crossed his arms over his chest. For a moment, he closed his eyes and inhaled deeply.

"I'm telling you this because —" Nash offered, carefully, "Look, I can provide some kind of reference but you know almost every interior designer in town. That will genuinely help her. Besides" Nash paused, giving him a long hard, look, "I thought you would want to know."

When Dev continued to remain silent, Nash added. "Dev, if this is still too hard for you, it's alright. I can..."

"No! That's not it." The urgency in his reply startled Nash.

The situation was so ridiculous in a twisted sense that a strangled, humorless laugh escaped from his lips. The heartbroken boy inside him wanted to blatantly walk away. It's not my problem. But Dev knew at once that he wouldn't be able to let go.

How hurtful it was to hear about her in this manner, as if she were just another story that was passed from one person to another? As if anyone else had the right to deal with her problems...

If he could help her? If? His mind, body and soul had been wired, a very long time ago, to care for her, even when she told him not to.

He shot up from his seat and dragged towards the large floor-ceiling window. Heavy clouds poured mercilessly over the city. "Why didn't she come to me?" he whispered, almost to himself.

Nash came to stand by him. Gently clapping one hand on his friend's shoulder, he said, "You can't expect her to just pick up the phone one evening and call you. Eight years is a long time."

"It shouldn't matter!" Dev interjected, loudly, with an emotion that wasn't directed at his friend. "She's been struggling and she found it easier to talk to some random person and not to me!" The hurt in his voice was unmistakable. His heart twisted in pain.

Nash dropped his hand and turned to fetch two fresh bottles of beer. He handed one to Dev and stood in silence, letting the moments pass.

Dev took a long gulp, his mouth relishing the bitterness from the beer. Somewhere in his mind, he realized, that his rage wasn't because she hadn't told him. It was because they had come to a point in their lives, when she no longer thought of calling him. There was a part of him that, against all reason, had believed that he still had the right to be the first one to know anything about her.

"We used to talk." Dev whispered. "Everyday. Every fucking day. No thought, no incident happened to just one of us." He gazed with disdain at the droplets streaming along the glass of the window. "Not once... not once, had I considered the possibility that I wouldn't hear her voice for years. It seemed impossible for my world to function without her. It seemed impossible that I could go on without her chattering beside me, always giving me far too many instructions than I needed. I wasn't prepared to develop this... this skill of learning to live without her. It was the hardest thing I've done so far. You know already. Our first year in college..." Dev closed his eyes, swallowing a hard, painful lump. There had been months of darkness...days when he would just stare at his phone waiting desperately for a reply. He had been drowning in alcohol and grief. His grades slipped in free fall as he was barely attending his classes. Had it not been for his two friends, he would've been kicked out of college in the very first year.

Nash who had been silent up to that point felt compelled to say, "We all have things that defeat us, at some point or another. It was a phase, Dev. Don't think about it. You've come a long way since."

Dev's breath slowed. He took another gulp. "I'll make some calls, reach out to a few people. Something will turn up, I'm sure. Once I have a lead, I'll send it to you. Give it to Sherman."

"I think you should talk to her directly."

A sad smile appeared on his face. "She won't talk to me."

"I don't want to get in the middle of this." Nash shook his head, uncomfortable. "It's not my place. I won't pretend to give a reference which is actually coming from you."

"I won't talk to her, Nash. I just can't." A dreadful, sinking feeling twisted in his chest. She had made it abundantly clear that there was no place for him in her life. Now to walk back on that road...he just didn't have the courage anymore.

"Figure a way out." Dev said, "Say whatever you want to Sherman. I won't do this myself."

Nash sighed, not the least bit happy.

Chapter 4

R ose was overjoyed. She couldn't believe that Matt had got her two interviews in less than a day.

"I can't thank you enough, Matt." Rose repeated. "You know someone at Ste. Clara Designs? God, why didn't you tell me sooner. They're such a fantastic design company. Even if I don't get the job, to be able to interview there is a huge deal for me."

Matt smiled. "Your welcome, Rose. But I think you should know, I cannot take all the credit. Nash Valani, the Willowbark architect you remember?"

"Yes, I remember." she said, quietly, her mind immediately going to the night of the party.

"He helped me a lot with the networking."

"How did Nash know I was looking for a job?" Rose asked, quietly.

"Oh, I asked him. Remember the party we went to last week. You left early for some reason. But I found out that Nash's old college mate is Dev Malhotra." Matt chuckled. "Can you believe it? I figured, now that's someone who can get you a good opportunity. So I asked Nash. Though," Matt paused, considering, "Nash was quite emphatic that Ste. Clara approached him for a reference."

"I see." Rose murmured.

"Did you know Morningstar Properties uses Ste. Clara a lot? It'll be great exposure for you. And honestly, now that I've connected with Nash, I'm hoping he'll convince someone at Morningstar to work with us. Hell, if that happens, I might be able to steal you back. Till then, you go ahead and gather your experience." Matt genuinely had her best interests at heart. She knew it. Which is why she smiled and didn't say anything right then.

She went home with a sense of forbearing. Thoughts stirred along, pricking at her conscience. Desperation fought with pride which fought with emotion

She was halfway through eating her take-out sandwich, when Samantha appeared looking worn out and irritated. Rose didn't say anything. It wasn't the first time Rose had seen Sam this way and this wouldn't be the last either. She watched as her roommate shrugged off her coat to reveal a mini skirt and a plunging tank top. Sam marched into her room and banged the door behind her. By the time she emerged, Rose was done with dinner and reclined on the patchy, coarse couch in their tiny living room.

"Bad day?" Rose asked, cautiously.

Sam was now wearing pajama shorts and a hoodie. Her makeup was cleaned off and hair wound in a loose ponytail. She joined Rose on the couch, dropping her head back. There was a loud gasp. Sam jumped from her seat. "Ow!" One palm clamped the back of her head.

"What happened!"

"Bloody spring! One just popped out right into my skull." The offensive spot on the couch received a strong smack. "Its falling apart already. We need to find a new one."

Rose groaned. With a lot of effort, a lot, they'd managed to haul this couch from a creepy woman's house across the street then vacuumed and cleaned it for hours. And it had barely been a few weeks.

"Let's just go to Ikea and get a new couch." Sam grumbled, resting her head back very slowly this time.

Rose dreaded accounting for another big expenditure. "Let me see if I can get some used floor model from one of the furniture suppliers."

Rose had met Sam through a Facebook page for Vancouver housing. At the time, Rose had been looking for a place which was moderately close to the city, walking distance to a metro station and most importantly, in her budget, which was meager at best. It was pure luck that Sam happened to be a great roommate and a wonderful person.

That is not to say, Sam didn't have her own problems. Far from it. She came from the bottom, right where people have to rely on food stamps and don't have enough to buy a new winter coat. She grew up watching her parents fight incessantly while her terrified little brother hid behind. Sheer courage and her own labors had made her survive. But beyond mere survival, her heart had managed to retain its kindness and her mind harbored a single dream - to go to medical school. She took classes at the community college, worked day and night, did everything under the sun, just to save up enough to attend a good university.

With genuine fondness, Rose said. "Talk to me, Sam. You'll feel better."

Sam turned her face sideways and gave Rose a tired smile. "A stupid man today tried to pull me in his lap."

Rose's eyes shot up, mouth parted in astonishment.

"Yeah, I know." Sam sighed. "It's fine though. I made sure all the drinks he ordered ended up on his stupid expensive suit."

"Your manager?"

"The man nearly passed out drunk so the manager just had him escorted out."

"And?"

"Nothing. My shift ended."

Rose frowned. "I really wish you would work somewhere else."

"Yeah, me too." Sam exhaled dramatically. "But honestly, this job pays very well. It would take me thrice as much time to earn that kind of cash anywhere else."

Sam worked part-time at Lobby77 an upscale lounge in downtown that asserted itself to be trendy and sophisticated. It wasn't. Behind it's stylish vibe was an unspoken understanding that the servers were there for pleasure. The later the night, the looser the guests became with maintaining decency. Subsequently, the servers were paid exceedingly well. For young men and women with a good face and an attractive body, it was nothing but fast cash.

"What happened with your job search? Did you boss help you out?" Sam asked.

"Yeah, kind of. But not really."

Sam chuckled dryly. "So no?"

Rose shook her head.

"Did you talk to your dad?" Sam asked.

"Yeah, a bit."

Through the years Rose had learnt to keep her father away from her financial troubles. Her dad's life was already a daily battle just to accept that his former days of glory were long gone. To add to it, his own health had been deteriorating. Now to hear that his only daughter lived in an apartment no bigger than a walk-in closet of her childhood home, would be pushing the aging gentleman to a breakdown. There was also the fact that every time Rose spoke to him, she was reminded that her father had gone from owning a construction company to doing minor remodeling jobs in the neighborhood.

"And your friend?" Sam asked, raising one eyebrow.

Through the course of the past couple of months, Rose and Sam had gotten close, sharing their life stories with one another. Rose had told her about Dev, or at least as much as her heart could share. Even before the night of the party, Sam had tried to suggest, more than once, that Rose should call him at least once since she was now in the same city.

"No, Sam. That ship has sailed. I can't talk to him." Rose replied, dejectedly. She bid Sam a good night and turned to her bedroom.

It was a small room with a twin bed, a square desk and a chair. To the corner stood a thin closet. Changing into her pajamas, she stepped into the shared bathroom. Her gaze stilled at her own reflection in the mirror.

Ever since she was a little girl, Rose had always believed that she was beautiful. Maybe it was her dotting mother had built a healthy self-esteem. At five-feet-three, she was shorter than the average but possessed a slender, feminine form. Her smooth brown locks fell past her shoulders, nearly touching her waist. Long curved eyebrows and a shapely nose. And her eyes - a fathomless ocean of blue, relentlessly absorbing every thing of beauty and intrigue. When she smiled those blue orbs glittered like liquid sapphires.

But Rose no longer smiled, not as much as she used to.

She blinked at her reflection and looked away, sighing. She no longer felt beautiful either.

There had been mistakes, plenty of them. And what she lived through now were the repercussions of those. She had no right to complain. All she could do was pay her dues and figure a way out of this mess, by herself.

The next day she called Matt. He did not take the news well.

"But, why?" Matt had asked, flabbergasted. "Why won't you apply?! You were so excited yesterday. Believe me, with the reference that Nash has given, your chances of landing the job are quite high.

"I need to take care of some family stuff." It was a lie.

"Think about it again, Rose. You told me yourself, you need this. It will really help with your debt situation."

"No, it wont." she whispered, quietly.

It would make it worse.

Chapter 5

Rose wanted to run away. This was hell.

Yanking the hem of her tiny skirt for the hundredth time, she balanced a tray of drinks. The relatively short walk to the table seemed to go on forever; her toes ached with each painful stride in heels that didn't qualify as shoes. She couldn't believe that this is what life had come to be.

Chin up, Rose. She persuaded herself. It's only temporary.

Setting the tray on the table she forced a smile, ignoring the way two sets of eyes openly gawked at her.

"Can I get you anything else, gentlemen?" She prayed that they didn't actually reply in the affirmative.

One of the guys shook his head and smiled at her, slow and leering. He reached to tap the back of her hand. It was a light touch but completely unnecessary. "Not at the moment. You can come back later."

Severely discomforted, she snatched her hand back suppressing the disgust that threatened to show on her face

"Rosie!" the manager hissed when she was one her way back to the bar to pick up another round of drinks.

"Yes, John?"

"Stop looking so damn skittish. Do we pay you to make the guests feel unwelcome?"

No, you don't. You pay me to tolerate actions that are fit for a strip club. she thought to herself. Yet, I'm here and I can't judge you because I really need the money.

Rose had not been able to find a job. Her work with Sherman hadn't been enough to showcase her talents. No one wanted to hire an inexperienced young woman who seemed so nervous during her interviews. She had finally managed to get a part-time sales job at a furniture store but there were bills to be paid, not to mention the debt interest alone had started haunting her dreams. In a moment of madness and desperation, Rose had asked Sam to get her a few shifts at Lobby77. This was the third night...of utter disaster. She couldn't get over the way men looked at her. The uniforms were appalling. It was shocking how the place flourished under the guise of being a trendy lounge when in reality it was nothing more than a sophisticated cover up for rich businessmen to pick up woman.

During her first shift, the manager had decided to call her Rosie.

"It's more...appealing." he had said.

And because she hated the job, she accepted the name without any resistance.

The next table she had to wait on, was occupied by a particularly nasty set of middle-aged men. She walked towards them with a heavy tray full of drinks and was about to set it on the table, when a hand touched the back of her thigh, creeping under her skirt. Instantly bewildered, the tray dropped from her hands propelling all the glasses in different directions. The contents spilled all over the guests and glasses crashed to pieces. It was a complete mess. The manager came running once again. He was already not impressed by her and such a commotion made him instantly angry.

All at once, the men started yelling while the manager shot her dirty looks. Another server appeared with two mops and promptly handed one to her. She cleaned the mess as quickly as possible and made herself invisible.

"Rose...just quit." Samantha came in behind her. "This isn't for you." She was used to her skimpy uniform and took a different name every other day. Today a small badge on the right of her crop top read, Mia.

"I need the money."

Sam's eyes furrowed. "I hate seeing you like this."

"You got used to it. So will I."

"There's a difference between you and me. I can deal with these things. You can't." Sam paused, biting her teeth, "And that's not criticism towards you."

Rose gave Sam a slow, meaningful look.

Why didn't the world realize, that behind every tough exterior is a wounded heart wallowing in the depths of yet another painful story.

"Don't try to imply that I'm better than this and that you're not." There was no way she was going to let her roommate feel inferior. Sam was her only friend, a truly warm human being amongst a sea of mean and selfish people. "Because that's not true! I shouldn't need to be doing this and neither should you. But here we are, anyway."

"Rose..."

She shook her head in dismissal. "Let's just get through the shift tonight."

"I'm actually going to be off in about thirty minutes. Do you want me to wait for you?"

"No...no. I still have two hours. You go home. Get some sleep. I'll see you in the morning."

After the mishap at the last table, Rose had assumed that the group would've asked for a different server. But they hadn't. Anxious and mortified, she found herself carrying another tray towards them, this time with appetizers.

"Darlin'" the man in the striped gray suit drawled. He was easily in his late forties or even early fifties and was giving her the look of a randy teenager. "You seemed a little nervous last time. Why don't we start over?"

Rose managed a weak smile and mumbled something to the effect that she was alright.

"What's your name, love?" The second man asked, clearly very drunk.

She stuttered and blurted. "Rosie."

"Ah..." the man in the gray suit exclaimed. "Such a sweet name for someone as beautiful as you."

The third man smirked. "Would you like to sit with us?"

"No, thank you. I should..." Rose swallowed, shuffling backward. "...go."

"We'll leave you a nice big tip. Don't worry. It'll be more than you get paid here for a week." The man continued condescendingly. "Come here."

He didn't wait for an answer. He reached forward and snatched her waist, yanking her into his lap. The other two men didn't react except to chuckle with approval.

She was so shocked that for a whole minute her body froze. Despite her troubles, in her life so far, she had always been safe. Within seconds three nobodies had shattered her sense of safety.

In the next heartbeat she fought out of his lap and turned to flee. The man however was egged on by her resistance.

"There... there, love. Easy now. We're just talking" His slimy hands found her waist again. It felt horrific. Any second now she was about to find herself back in his lap and...

It never happened.

The man's hands were yanked away, making her recoil several inches.

A tall male figure in a pitch black suit had put himself in front of her.

"Get your fucking hands off her!"

She didn't need to see his face. The sound of his voice - deep and masculine that now raged with something dark and dangerous - had the ability to pull her back to life from the deepest state of unconsciousness. The smell of cedar wood and forest invaded her senses.

Amidst the miserable chaos of her current predicament a feeling of certainty arose. She was sure, as sure as one is of the rising sun, nothing would touch her. Not anymore.

Her world was safe again.

He was here.

Chapter 6

"N ot bad, Malhotra" Max Stanley smirked with approval. "Your city has something fun to do after all. We were starting to get bored."

Dev chuckled dryly. Maneuvering his way through the dimly lit, fairly crowded space of Lobby77, he headed to their table. Three investment bankers were visiting from New York. They weren't directly conducting business with Dev but it was only polite to entertain them while they were here.

A female server appeared at their table. She wore the standard uniform, a short black skirt and a skimpy crop top with a plunging neckline and introduced herself as Mia. It was obviously not her real name. She must've been experienced at her job with a skill to smell out desperation. Because when she bent to pick up the menus, she made sure to let Max get a longer glance at her chest.

The conversation, inadvertently, turned towards business and Dev was starting to get intrigued by some of the stories they told him. The server reappeared carrying a tray with their drinks when a sudden loud explosion stilled everyone around. There were gasps followed by quick and intense yelling.

"Oh no!" Mia groaned, looked behind them at the source of all the noise. "Again?"

Dev turned to look in the direction of her vision.

For the second time, in a month, he found himself wrought with shock. This time was worse, however because his shock was superseded by fury. Dressed in that obnoxious uniform, her terrified eyes staring at the mess of broken glass, was the girl who had haunted his dreams for weeks.

"New girl?" Ali watched as the manager rushed in.

"Third shift...still hasn't got her groove yet." Mia shook her head sympathetically.

"If I had to wait on those shriveled creeps, I wouldn't find my grove either." Max exclaimed. Ali and Wesley sniggered.

Mia smiled dryly and withdrew the empty tray. "Almost makes me regret getting her the job."

"Why did you then?" Dev demanded, completely out of line.

Mia's eyes narrowed, not appreciating his tone. "Because she needed the money"

"I'd like to meet her." Max winked at Mia. "I can think of plenty activities that I'll happily pay her for."

Dev shut his eyes forcing himself to stay seated. Every fiber in his body wanted to lunge forward and punch Max. The night became disastrous after that. Wesley asked if Dev was feeling well since he'd suddenly quietened.

"I'm starting to get a headache." he muttered.

It wasn't a complete lie. He barely touched his drinks. Instead, he watched, painstakingly, as Rose walked around in indecent heels, tugging at her tiny skirt every now and then. When she bent lower to set plates or glasses, one hand instinctively reached to readjust that ridiculous neckline of the top.

Dev had made up his mind - at the end of the night, he was going to talk to her.

However, that resolve was quickly broken when one of the men pulled her into his lap. It was pure instinct followed by an involuntary series of movements that led him to step in front of her.

"Get your fucking hands off her!" he bellowed.

Before anyone had any time to respond, Dev had punched the man who had grabbed her, causing him to collapse on the floor. That, in Dev's opinion, was his best attempt at restrain. In his mind, he had wanted to do worse... much worse.

"How dare you!" A second man yelled. The injured fellow struggled to get back on his feet, angry and disoriented. A dark bruise was already emerging on one side of his cheek.

Dev's friends came rushing to the scene followed promptly by the manager.

"Sir...Sir..." the manager grappled, trying to calm the older and the younger man who were staring daggers at each other.

"What is the meaning of this?!" The third man demanded of the manager. "We were just trying to have a friendly conversation with the server. Is that a crime now?"

"Yes, of course, Sir. There seems to be some misunderstanding." The manager turned to Dev but quickly backed off once he recognized him.

Dev looked frightful, intimidating and unstable. Barely aware of the simpering manager or the other men around, he was staring a hole at the bastard who had touched her.

Teach him a lesson. The devil inside him hissed. No one touches her! A few broken bones... that should do it. Dev's fingers curled into a fist. His breathing was heavy and labored, fighting the violent thoughts in his head. A second bruise on the other side will even out his dirty face. It'll remind him never to even look at your Rose again...

"Dev. Let it go, mate. It's not worth it." Max touched his shoulder with caution.

"Gentlemen." The manager tried with commendable diplomacy. "This is all a misunderstanding. Let's take a step back." He looked over Dev's shoulder and bit between his teeth. "Go inside, Rosie."

Before she could move, Dev's voice resonated.

"Wait." He ordered and for a moment no one moved.

His eyes remained on the injured man so it became uncertain to whom the command was directed at. But Rose knew he was talking to her. She looked up at him. His face was stone hard, mouth closed severely.

Don't do anything. She pleaded silently. Let me go.

"This silly girl ruined our entire evening!" The injured man interjected. Rose winced, deeply worried that the if the stupid man continued, there would be no telling what Dev would do.

The second man waved angrily, "You're running this overpriced, fancy excuse for a club and you hire a stupid chit."

Dev growled. He was about to lunge forward but to his regret, his eyes fell on Rose again. She was terrified and silently shaking her head. He glared at her, but remained still.

"Put their check on my tab." Dev snapped to the manager.

The injured man huffed indignantly. "You think I can't afford to pay for my own drinks, foolish boy? This isn't about money. I want to see some accountability here."

"Sir, we're more than happy to take care of your bill for tonight." The manager supplied, then threw a worried glance at Dev. "I mean both your checks."

"That's not the point." the man barked, completely unaware that his safety was balanced on the rickety edge of Dev's restraint. "This little bi..."

"Shut the fuck up, old man." Dev snarled in a low whisper. Bringing himself to his full height, he took two steps ahead. All the three men visibly cowered. "Before I give you a real reason to complain."

The man gaped, speechless. "How dare you talk to me like that? I'm going to get your arrested." Wesley and Max exchanged a dubious glance. The man was drunk enough to make such ludicrous statements. Didn't he realize who he was talking to?

"Are you going to call the cops?" Dev mocked, his eyes bright and menacing. "Go ahead."

"No!" The manager blurted. One cop is all it would take to shut down his whole place. At least for a few days till his superiors bribed the right kind of people once again. "I mean, let's just..."

"Do you know who I am?" The man boasted in attempt to intimidate. "I know the owner of this place. I'm going to..."

Dev laughed, humorless and dark. "Fantastic idea. Call him."

The man eyes widened, dumbfounded. "What?"

"Call. him. Do it now. And while you're at it, say hi to my father. They're having dinner together. At my father's house."

Dev hated using his family connections like a bratty teenager but sometimes to deal with menacing idiocy, one has to respond in a language that can be understood loud and clear.

The other two men spoke in hushed voices, urging their companion to back down. Dev's friends had stepped forward whispering suggestions and discreetly signaling to the manager.

"Rosie! Go." The manager hissed, desperate to wrap this chaos.

But Rose remained rooted to the spot.

Dev knew the only way to stop himself from punching that bastard again was to leave.mHe turned and went towards her. She peered up at him. Deep lines ran along her forehead and her eyes were filled with fear and shame. He blinked and exhaled a heavy breath, controlling the urge to turn around. Then his fingers closed around her elbow and without missing a beat, he dragged her away from the entire fiasco. The audience was rendered speechless. But Rose wasn't paying them any attention.

It was the first time he had touched her...in eight years.

Heat ignited at her elbow, spreading through her body like wild fire. Her eyes were on him as he marched ahead. She opened and closed her mouth several times trying to say a word but nothing came out.

"Where are your things?" he asked, brazenly walking into the door that said, Employees Only.

His hand was so warm. It covered only the span of her elbow but it felt like he had enveloped her whole body in his arms.

"Rose?" he prodded.

She stretched one hand, pointing to the far left, her eyes never leaving his. His hand dropped from her elbow. All at once an iciness crept inside her body.

"Get your things."

"Dev..."

With two fingers and his thumb, he pressed between his brows and shut his eyes for a moment. "Get your things. Now."

She was tired and hurt and just wanted this disastrous night to end. With quiet movements, she scurried to the corner and grabbed her bag. When she returned within minutes, a gray woolen coat was buttoned neatly over her and the heels had been replaced with short winter boots.

The manager rushed in, livid and ready to yell. "Rosie, what the..."

Before he could even get close, the six foot seething male had once again stepped in between, hiding Rose behind his shoulder.

"She quits." Dev said, his tone flat and unyielding. He wrapped one hand around her waist and pulled her away. Just before the door closed behind them, he threw an angry glance at the manager, "And don't ever call her Rosie."

Dev's colleagues had rushed in to show their genuine concern. They had summarized that the waitress meant something to him. He responded hastily telling them he would call them tomorrow and strode to the parking lot with one hand firmly around Rose.

It was brash - he knew.

He was hauling her like a rough, ill-mannered brute - he knew.

The situation could've been resolved with more pragmatism - he knew!

But a dormant sense of possessiveness had overtaken him. He hadn't thought it possible that he should still feel this violently protective of her. It was no longer important that she didn't want his help. He was damn well not going to leave her alone. Anger had been replaced with fury...fury at the world which had brought this girl to such a state. His breathing drew deeper, his jaw clenched and his other hand curled into a tight fist.

Didn't these people realize who she was? How could the world not know? This girl wasn't just anyone... She wasn't a mere friend or an old neighbor - No. Hell, she wasn't even the girl he had once 'liked' - No!

After all these years, the truth had remained unchanged.

Rose Barnes was Dev Malhotra's pride. And no one, absolutely no one, dare hurt his Pride.

Chapter 7

"Where's your car?" Dev asked. The black BMW in front of them flashed once when he unlocked it.

"I took the SkyTrain."

He scowled. "Fine. I'll drop you home."

"No!" she blurted very loudly, "I mean, there's no need. The station is just round the corner and the train is quite comfortable."

"It's past midnight. You're not taking the train alone now."

"I've done it plenty of times."

"I'm not asking." he snapped. Without pausing, he got into the driver seat. Strapping the seat belt, he lowered the passenger side window and looked at her. "Come on, Rose. You're acting like a child."

Rose gaped. "I'm...I'm..." she sputtered, "You are the one acting like a child...a crazy child! I'm still in shock about what happened upstairs. You actually punched..." she blinked in disbelief, "what if someone calls the cops on you."

"No one up there is that stupid." He raked one hand through his hair. "Now get in the car."

"Look, you don't need to go through the trouble." she said, hurriedly. "I'll call you tomorrow and maybe we can meet later..."

A doubt emerged in his mind. It was the way she was reacting, there was some level fear behind her words. "Rose..."

"No." she whispered, shaking her head.

He glared at her, his patience at an end. "If you don't get into the fucking car right now, I will bodily shove you in."

She gaped in shock. Surely he was bluffing. He gave her a sharp look, one eyebrow raised in warning. When she didn't move, he unbuckled the seat belt and reached for the door.

"Fine! Fine." she raised her hands defensively, feet shuffling quickly.

She took a seat on the passenger side and complied with reluctance when he asked her to type her address on the navigation screen in front of them.

They drove in silence. Every now and then when some external light flashed through the window, his attention was drawn to her exposed thighs. He gripped the steering wheel tighter. To comment on someone's choice of clothing, especially a woman's, was not in his nature but the fact that she had been visibly disturbed in that tiny skirt made him angrier.

When he took the exit prompted by the navigation the change in the neighborhood was impossible to miss. He understood at once why she had been so opposed to the idea of him driving her home. She didn't want him to see this.

The streets were dirty and ragged. Trash lay all around and not a wall was left bare; graffiti was splashed everywhere. When he pulled into the parking lot of her apartment building, Rose braved a glance at him and wasn't at all surprised to see a scowl on his face. He remained silent, looking straight ahead with an indescribable expression. The building was old and worn beyond repair. Dark, loud graffiti covered one wall against which, a small group of badly dressed guys were smoking what was clearly not a cigarette. They gave Dev a good idea of the kind of people residing there.

His calm was more dangerous than any angry words he could've given. He got out of the car and walked around to open her door. "Let's go." His voice so cold, it made her heart drop.

They took the shabby stairs to the fifth floor.

"The elevator is broken" she mumbled.

With trembling hands, she produced a set of keys from her purse and opened the front door. He stepped into the living room or rather the tiny rectangular space that was occupied with a shoddy worn out couch pushed against the wall by a small window. Adjacent to it was a small circular table with two mismatched chairs. The kitchen was a tiny corner to the right of the entrance.

When Rose turned to look up at him, her eyes grew wide. During their walk upstairs she had sensed and readied herself to face his anger. But what she saw now was beyond that.

Torture. The man looked tortured.

In sheer irony, she began to explain; not to defend herself but to calm him down.

"It's not that bad." she started, forcing herself to remain steady and non-chalant. "My roommate's a nice girl. You met her. She was waiting on you at the club. Mia? Actually her name is Samantha. I get along with her very well. The neighbors aren't too bad either. The metro station is right behind so I don't even have to walk." She was rambling but he hadn't moved a muscle, or even blinked so she felt compelled to go on. "Honestly, I'm hardly home. I work on most weekends too so I'm just here to sleep and eat breakfast."

He took a step forward. Without any reason, she stumbled back hitting one of the dining chairs. He was glaring at her and for a moment it seemed like he was going to yell. With an abruptness that was startling, he pivoted on his heel.

"Wait, that's Samantha's room. Mine is..."

He promptly changed his course and marched into the opposite room. Every piece of furniture was mismatched giving the distinct impression that it was used or maybe even found somewhere lying about. His hand shot up, fingers running through his hair. He wouldn't forget this sight for a long, long time. This is where she's been living. He told himself, letting the words serve as self punishment. While he was out there, getting mad at her because his ego felt bruised, she had been slogging away in this god-for-saken hole. How Dev had managed to remain calm, was astounding to say the least.

"Dev," She whispered a feeble plea, standing inches away.

He looked down into her eyes, blue orbs now filled with fear and sadness. Her soft lips were shaped so delicately that it made the contradiction of the disaster around even more horrible. The long shapely eyebrows, the curve of her cheek that culminated into the slanting angle of her jaw. He hadn't forgotten a single detail.

The years and the miles meant nothing. Her face was committed into the memory of his soul.

It was this - this exquisite, innocent, beautiful face of hers set against the background of a miserable excuse of a home that made his torture more excruciating.

"Say something," she whispered.

When she was almost sure he wasn't going to answer, he ordered, quietly. "Pack a bag."

She backed away, thoroughly befuddled. Before any defenses could come out of her mouth, he had charged to the tiny closet and had begun to randomly snatch pieces of clothing.

"What are you doing!" her voice hoarse with shock.

"Helping you," another hanger was flung across to meet the small pile on the bed, "pack."

Her brain was surely muddled because she blurted, senselessly, "You're making a mess."

"There isn't enough to make a bloody mess here."

"Stop." she yelped clutching at his arms but he simply shrugged like she was a pesky fly.

He felt entitled to his authority, as if it was perfectly normal for him to step into her personal space and decide the course of her actions. As if they were simply standing in her old bedroom, far away in Aspen Gardens, and arguing over something silly. As if the eight years hadn't taken place. Anger rose inside her because she realized she felt the same.

Even so his behavior was ridiculous and she was in no mood to excuse it. With a strength that came from a mix of anger and adrenaline, she jumped in front of him, slammed both her hands on his chest and gave a hard push.

It wasn't the impact, which despite her best effort did not cause him any pain, it was the surprise that stilled him. His gaze bore into hers.

An instant is all it took to realize that she had made a mistake.

He jumped, twisting her around till her back collided with the wall, pinning her with his body. His free hand slammed past her head on the wall beside, palm flat, the lines of his forearm strained and solid. His face was only inches away from hers.

The sequence spanned for barely three seconds but it knocked the air right out of her chest. The frame of his body caged her, hard muscle contradicting the warmth radiating from it. Her elbows were bent to the sides, two small fists separating their chests. But she couldn't conjure enough strength to fight him again. Her mind was occupied with a glaring memory. Their last good bye, just before he'd left for college. They'd been in the similar position with the same underlying emotion.

Except...

Back then, that eighteen-year-old boy had left. Now, this all-consuming man was holding her in a death-grip. The skies above wouldn't have dared to wrench her out of his arms. Even she had lost the power to move.

She'd never been held, not like this. Dominance thrills the body for a short while then wears off fairly easily to show its ugly head. This wasn't dominance. This was pure male strength. The kind that is resolute, austere with an unshakeable integrity at it's core. His fingers dug into her skin, steely and harsh but not painful, not even for a second. She knew that he would destroy the world, his own included, before causing her pain. And maybe she'd always known it...even when they were young and unwise to understand these things.

"Dev..." she murmured, as if his name held in itself every emotion of her heart.

Her face was tipped upward inadvertently drawing his eyes to the slender column of her neck; the elegant expanse of skin teasing him. He swallowed hard, the swell of his Adam's apple rising and falling. Just a taste. The devil murmured in his mind. Just one taste to see if she's as sweet. No more. A kiss won't hurt anyone.

"I won't let you stay here." he murmured, hollow and unyielding.

"I've..." she began but words were lodged somewhere in her throat. Drawing in a deep breath, she continued, quietly. "I've been living here for five months."

"And you will not remain for another five minutes."

Her fists were half curled, half clutching at the fabric of his shirt. His face hovered an inch overs hers. She considered the possibility that he might kiss her. And it terrified her, in the very next instant, that the first thought to that possibility was not resistance but intrigue.

But the touch never came.

"Listen to me carefully." His words stung against her mouth, "You're coming home with me. I'm not asking. I'm not debating. It's non-negotiable." He watched with satisfaction as some level of fear entered in her eyes. Good, he thought. She needs to understand. "I will not go back to the forty-second floor of my three-bedroom apartment, knowing that this is where you will be sleeping tonight. So Rose," even the venom in his voice couldn't mask the agony of his heart, "you have two minutes to pack a bag and leave with me before I completely lose my mind."

Chapter 8

Dev drove through the relatively empty freeway, Rose quiet beside him. She'd changed into a pair of knit tights, a brown sweatshirt and short winter boots. It considerably lightened his anger.

"Dev?" Her small voice echoed in the rumbling silence between them.

"Hmm..."

"I'm hungry."

He glanced at her, but she was turned the other way, looking out the window.

"Alright." he replied, softly.

It was one in the morning. Their only option would be a drive-thru, which neither of them minded. He took the exit leading to his apartment but made a detour to an A&W.

Before she could even look at the menu, he turned to her to ask, "Spicy chicken burger?"

"Um...yeah." There was no need to actually answer. It's what she always ordered at any drive-thru.

He lowered his window. "Two spicy chicken burgers."

"Three" she interrupted. When he glanced at her, she supplied, "I'm very hungry."

Despite the heaviness of the entire night, his lips pursued into a ghost of a smile. "Make that three burgers. Fries?" he asked her the last part.

She shook her head.

Shortly after, she found herself stepping into Dev's high-rise condo. The entryway was narrow but organized neatly with a plain bench in natural wood and black hooks at the top. It led her into a modern kitchen with high end appliances. There was a marble counter top in the center and bar stools tucked underneath it. A round dining table surrounded by four beige fabric chairs lay beyond. The living area consisted of a long gray couch, a rectangular coffee table and two arm chairs on the other side. To the right, a path led toward the bedrooms. All around the walls, tasteful pieces of artwork and picture frames were spread in perfect harmony. Bringing in all these elements together, in a theme of sheer grandeur were the massive floor-to-ceiling windows that spread across one entire wall.

The space screamed of luxury, comfort, style and a promise of a long successful journey ahead.

"You own this? she asked, though she already knew the answer.

"Yes.".

It had been uncomfortable to stand with him in her shabby, broken apartment. But now surrounded by such wealth and luxury she felt completely out of place. The burst of twinkling city lights beckoned her towards the window. She took cautious steps toward it. A gasp left her lips at the view that lay ahead.

It was breathtaking. The entire Vancouver skyline in a single, sweeping image.

Dev had always considered this view as the focal point of his home. It had been the primary reason to buy the condo. He had spent numerous mornings and even more evenings watching the seasons play out on. Some days the sun drowned the city in it's bright warmth. Other days, like tonight, the clouds roared in all their splendor. Once a year, the city was obscured by a blanket of sparkling snowflakes. The seasons came by but the view beyond his home remained constant in it's theme of beauty.

Until this moment.

This woman, with her wavy brown hair, was doing something peculiar to the view outside, simply by standing in front of it. He strained to under-stand at first. But as she remained there longer, her back to him, realization creeped in. The shape of her body, the curve of her waist, the locks of hair which, from a distance, seem to cut through the glass in tantalizing waves - it all had one purpose...

The purpose being to render the focal point into a mere backdrop for her own phenomenal beauty. Gently, unintentionally, she had pushed the Vancouver skyline out of focus.

He would never be able to look out his window that same way again. She had proved to him that no matter how high his home might be elevated or how broad his horizon might stretch, she would always be his focus.

"This is magnificent," she murmured after a long time.

"Yes, it is." he replied, eyes on her, unwavering.

She turned sideways, resting against the window frame. Her mind felt uncertain, distracted and sad. "I lost the job."

"I know."

"I would've continued working there had you not shown up."

"I know."

"I hated that job."

He leaned in and spoke softly. "I know."

"I need to find something else. I have to pay rent and..."

"You aren't going back to that apartment."

She turned to face him. "That it not for you to decide."

"It isn't." He stated, evenly. "But I'm deciding nonetheless."

"It does not work that way."

"You can counter me for the rest of night. It won't change my mind."

Frustration and dread filling her. "None of this is making any sense. I don't know what I'm doing here. I don't know why I agreed to come. I don't know why I listened to you in the first place. I shouldn't be here." Raising one arm, she jabbed an index finger toward the open city. "I should be there, doing what needs to be done to survive. But I'm here and my brain is no longer functioning."

His face was hard and impassive. "Let's eat first."

They ate in silence and quickly. The speed with which Rose devoured one burger then the next made it fairly obvious that she had missed more than just dinner.

When they retreated into the living room, Dev spoke as though he had been holding himself all this while, "You have a lot of explaining to do, Barnes."

She took a seat on the couch, staring at the floor.

"Are you going to volunteer to begin?" He asked, standing ahead, arms crossed over his chest. "No? Alright. Let's go through this one question at a time...

"Why were you living in that hell hole?"

She didn't reply.

"Why were you working at Lobby77?"

She blinked.

"Why did I find you in a slutty uniform being groped by a nasty old man?"

Silence. His anger derailed at a frightening pace.

"And for fuck sake, why haven't you told me any of this before?"

There were no easy answers to his questions. They both knew that.

He made an accusatory gesture with one arm, staring down at her with menacing coldness. "Do you have any idea, any fucking idea, how I felt when that lecherous bastard had put his hands on you? I was this close," he displayed an inch of air between his index finger and thumb, "this close to breaking all his bones. And the amazing part of it is, he was only doing what every man does in that place."

He raked one hand through his hair. For a man who prided himself on maintaining composure, he was shockingly out of control. "I don't understand why you were working there in the first place. You cannot possibly be so fucking naive not to understand the kind of service those servers have to provide. Are you stupid, Rose? Huh? The environment you put yourself into...are you aware how dangerous it was? Did you consider, even once, that what happened tonight was probably best case scenario for that job?"

The torrent of angry words didn't end for several minutes. He went on pointing out in different ways how careless she had been about her safety. She listened quietly. Her own despair momentarily forgotten. Had anyone else raised their voice and questioned her in this manner, she would've walked out after the first sentence. But Dev wasn't just anyone.

His eyes were shot with rage as if her actions had caused him pain.

But they had...a different kind of pain.

"When did you move to Vancouver?" he demanded.

She didn't want to tell him.

"I asked you a question."

"Five months." she murmured, preparing herself for further disapproval.

"Five...Five..." He stopped short with incredulous fury. Closing his eyes, he took long breaths. "You're mad at me, I get. I fucking get it! But that is no reason to go and sabotage your own safety. You've been here five months, in that fucking apartment and you didn't think of telling me about it!" He stepped back and turned sideways. "Fuck, Rose... why!" There was less anger now and more pain. He had taken off his jacket and folded the sleeves of his black shirt. His disheveled state made him look even more intimidating.

Her eyelids fell with shame and embarrassment. "I didn't think you would ever want to see me...and at that party last month, you were so angry..."

"So you decided to wait till I go completely mad?"

She looked at him, wounded and anxious. "You broke a glass..."

"You once broke my bedroom window, on purpose, just because I refused to drive you to some stupid concert during finals week."

"Dev..." she replied, feebly. "After everything I did, I couldn't possibly..."

"But I told you!" His face snapped to her, "I told you I would always be there. You just had to call."

"And say what? 'Dev, we haven't spoken a word in eight years but you see my life has screwed me over. So can you leave everything and come and help me?'"

"All you had to do was call me, even if it was after eight years, and say, come and get me."

A sad chuckle left her lips. "Really? And what after that?"

"Depending on where I was while reading your message, I would've been at your doorstep anywhere from a few minutes to a couple of hours."

"I wish if it were that simple." A rueful smile appeared on her face.

"It is."

"No, Dev, it's not. It's one thing to say something that...nice, but it won't change reality. My life is a complete chaos and it's no one's fault but my own." She pressed a palm to her forehead, trying to soothe her exhaustion. "So much has happened. I don't think I have the strength to discuss it all today."

Dev's jaw clenched tightly. He blinked, trying to regain some composure. The winds picked up momentum making the surrounding cold. He walked to slide the windows onto the other side, closing them, cutting off the sounds of the city.

"Go to bed." His voice had lost emotion. "Get some rest."

"Here... in your house." It wasn't a question, just a statement to make herself believe it.

"Yes, here. I have two spare rooms," he pointed to the left of the kitchen. "Take your pick. If you need anything my room is just across over there." he indicated to the doorway leading to the opposite side.

She nodded and advanced to pick up her duffle bag that he'd set aside. Before disappearing into the doorway, she glanced back. He was standing by the closed window - his body tall and lean, wide shoulders rolled back, feet braced apart and one hand inside his pocket. Gone was the confused, aimless kid who'd followed her around all those years ago. The man who stood in front of her now exuded a kind of strength which had only been a feeble promise in his youth.

"Dev." Her throated hurt but she forced herself to produce the words. "Thank y..."

"Don't." He interjected before she could complete. There was only so much he could take in one night. "Don't say it. Go to sleep, Ro."

When her head hit the pillow, a teary smile spread across her face.

Chapter 9

- -

Back then -

Aspen Gardens was a quiet suburb tucked away in the south of Edmonton, Alberta. Daniel Barnes had inherited his father's construction business and had made a reputable name for himself. He married a bright, young interior designer and when they're daughter Rose was born, he expanded his small family home into a stunning suburban mansion.

Across from them resided an Indian family in a modest home. Diljeet and Ranjeet Malhotra, newly arrive immigrants lived with their families. With an exorbitant amount of hard work, they had set up their own small but respectable construction business. The Malhotra family was, in a word - guarded. They lived peacefully, respectfully but kept themselves largely discreet. As first generation immigrants, their sense of social bonding was overtly cautious, especially when it came to their children.

It was Rose's mother, Catherine, who had first walked up to their house, her twelve-year-old daughter in tow. She found an unexpected bond with Ranjeet's wife, Anjali. They were closer in age, their first burns in the same grade and both had an avid interest in interior design. The affection flowed naturally to their children. Friday evenings Rose had samosas at the

Malhotras and Saturday mornings Dev and his younger sister, Anandita -
'Annie' - sat with the Barnes for pancakes.

It was common amongst Indian families to refer to a friend's mother as
'Auntie' even if they weren't directly related. It was a sign of respect and
familial affection. And so the mothers became Cathy Auntie and Anjee
Auntie to each others kids. It was these small, simple, routine things that
solidified the bond between the mothers and their children.

Rose and Dev became two names that were no longer pronounced sepa-
rately.

"Rose and Dev are going to the park."

"Rose and Dev are on their way to school"

"Rose and Dev are always late."

"Rose, Dev is here..."

"Dev, Rose is waiting..."

"Rose and Dev..."

It was always ever Rose and Dev. One never without the other.

Dev's upbringing in India had been filled with comfort and luxury. He
went to the best schools and grew up with an army of cousins and friends.
But suddenly finding himself in a different country, the twelve-year old
boy's confidence dwindled. He was terrified on his first day at his new
school. There were very few students of color at that time. Everyone was
different and they all knew each other in some capacity.

Rose walked right beside him, each step of the way. She held his hand,
sometimes quite literally, and helped him navigate the complicated school
rules and subtle nuances social interaction. She introduced him to all her

friends, signed him up for events and pushed him to take talk to other boys. Slowly, he relaxed. He got into the football team and began to smile a little.

Within months most of his classmates and teachers realized that Dev was actually very intelligent. Rose's own math accomplishments were just average. Dev was expert! Especially at calculus and physics. He found history and literature difficult but he was eager to learn and had no qualms about admitting his lack of knowledge. Rose liked that best about him. He tutored her rigorously to improve her calculus but never once made her feel like she wasn't as good as he was. He simply asked her to help him with history.

With good grades and stellar performance for the football team, Dev began to find his place and made his own friends too. But through it all, Rose was always the first person he turned to, the first person he wanted to talk to. She was like no one he'd ever known. Her spirit was extravagant. Everything she liked had to be amazing, phenomenal and out of the ordinary. She always wanted to try something new - the new movie, the new ice cream, the new sneakers, the new everything. Beneath all the energy, lay a soft girl with a kind and generous heart. She rescued stray animals and participated in city wide recycling drives. She was always a bit more polite to girls younger than her. More than once, she had come to Annie's rescue at school, when the younger girl had found herself in stressful situations.

During summers their mothers often took them to the beach. They built castles, entire cities in the sand, shaping them with their small hands and big dreams.

"Let's try to find seashells that can match our eyes." Rose quipped one afternoon. They were around fourteen and out on the beach with their moms and the rest of the Malhotra kids.

Dev scrunched his nose. "What kind of a game is that?"

"It'll be fun!" Rose pulled at his arm, dragging him toward the gentle waves. Dev grudging agreed. That was the problem, he could never say no to her, no matter how silly or whimsical he found her ideas to be. If he said no, she would pout and her eyes would become round and glassy, and Dev would feel like horrible inside.

They spent a good twenty minutes scurrying about, digging here and there, plucking out shells and pebbles. Dev, feeling triumphant, produced a nice rounded seashell with bright specks of blue. Rose on the other hand found one which was rather odd with blots of muddy brown.

"Seriously? This is what you found?" Dev frowned.

"It's perfect. I'm keeping it." She closed her palm around it and pressed her fist to her chest. Dev had felt a little irritated that she thought his eyes looked muddy and bland. Rose, on the other hand, had gone home pleased with herself; she had found the most unique seashell from the whole beach.

At his core, Dev was immensely protective. At first his protectiveness was limited to his younger sister, who was somehow having a harder time in her new life. But gradually, it extended to Rose. Even at that young age he was cognizant of the fact that Rose shouldn't be left alone late in the evenings or in certain parts of the city. He made sure to drop her home while she chattered beside him, blissfully oblivious.

Someone teased her at school once, calling her Rosie. She hated the name and tried to say so but the boy continued. Even though the boy was older and bigger, Dev stepped ahead. He stood firm, covering Rose behind his shoulder.

"Don't worry, Ro." he emphasized the right nickname, his voice cold and deceptively calm. "No one's going to dare call you that again. Isn't that right?" His eyes were burning a hole into that boy's head, causing him to swallow with fear.

No one called her Rosie after that.

They had foolishly climbed a tree once. Rose wanted to pursue a kitten or a squirrel or whatever moving entity that had caught her fascination. Dev had followed, reluctantly and mostly just to make sure she didn't fall. But they did fall. Dev caught her at the last instant, taking the fall himself. Not a single scratch came on her. He had to wear a sling on his left arm for a month.

Rose, like her own mother, had found a love for design. She loved to paint, draw, go to museums and read books. She created massive installations for school events, painted murals for the city fundraising projects and filled up streets with chalk-art during the children's summer camp. Her mind exploded with bright and creative ideas.

It was inevitable that he had a crush on her.

It was just a small crush at first, that instant rush of excitement whenever she appeared. But as they spent more time together his feelings deepened. Gradually he got the distinct impression that she felt the same. They sat closer to each other. Touches grew easy and familiar, or maybe that had always been the case; they were only just becoming more aware of it. She put his head on his shoulder as they spent ideal hours reclining on their oak tree.

They spent a lot of time on their oak tree.

In the middle of an open green field, a massive oak sprung from the ground. From afar it looked like a ladder connecting the earth to the skies. Rose and Dev spend their teenage years under the comfortable shade of it's sprawling branches. During the summer, when the fields turned more yellow than green, they played, read, lounged, did homework, talked about important things, silly things and nothing at all.

"Let's race!" Rose announced on day. They'd been sprawled on the grass, immersed in reading assignments for hours.

Dev agreed to the race but disagreed to the starting command.

"It's Ready, Steady, Go!" Rose explained, patiently.

"No, Ro. It's On you mark, Get set, Go!" he replied with slow emphasis.

She frowned. "But I've always done Ready, Steady, Go."

"And I've always done, On your mark, Get set, Go." he replied, haughtily.

"That's too many words!" She stomped one foot.

He chuckled, enjoying the way her nose crinkled in annoyance. "Hardly. You just want to do it your way." His accent had faded. Sometimes his A's and V's were a bit different, but it had become increasingly hard to tell that he'd spent his boyhood in a different country.

She crossed her arms over her chest and thought for a long moment. Her eyes narrowed at the Oak tree far ahead, squinting, as if assessing the distance. "Okay." she said, her brows relaxing. "We'll do it your way."

They picked an arbitrary line in front of them and got into a running stance.

He threw a glance at her. "I'm going to win, you know?"

Even though they both knew he was faster than her, she didn't care for his arrogance at that moment. "We'll see." she muttered, a cryptic smirk on her face.

"On your mark." He turned his focus back ahead. "Get set."

She set off!

Ignoring his angry protests, she ran as fast as her feet could take her. Her pace quickened. The oak tree was closer now. She was nearly there when he dashed past her, reaching the trunk first. They fell to their knees, catching their breaths.

"That's cheating." he accused, even though he had won.

She laughed, boastful and arrogant. "Yes. What are you going to do about it?"

Dev stared at her and realized he was mesmerized. A red flush at appeared on her face, she was still breathless and her hair had come lose from it's simple ponytail. He didn't understand what he felt in that moment but he knew somewhere deep down that she would never be just his friend.

Shaking his head, he got up.

"You want to race back?" she asked, cheekily.

"Shut up." He was already walking. "Let's get back to work."

Chapter 10

Back then -

By the time they were sixteen, conversations turned largely toward college and plans for the future. Years of creative projects had made it easy for Rose to find her calling

"Design school." she announced one fine day. "I think I want to get into interior designing."

"Makes sense." Dev nodded, unsurprised by her declaration. "You have a natural talent for it."

She beamed. His compliments meant more to her than grades and outer accolades. "Have you decided yet?" she asked, delicately. When he didn't reply, a sad frown appeared on her face. "You have to trust your instinct, Dev. You need to start preparing now if you want to get into the right school."

They were sitting in the library. His elbows rested on the table, palms against his forehead, fingers wound in his hair. "I don't know." he muttered under his breath.

It was time to pick electives, seek internships and experiences that could prepare him for college. Instead, Dev found himself in the middle of complete indecision. His father wanted him to pick a business major and go to one of the top schools in the US. Their construction business was growing. The senior Malhotra brothers were exploring opportunities in the British Columbia, Washington and California, making assessments as to which would help them grow their wealth. Though their own lifestyles were innately humble, they were discreetly saving up large college funds for their children.

Dev had no interest in business school. Being with Rose had made him appreciate the arts but he wasn't an artist either nor did he have any creative inclination. He had some interest in architecture and a little in engineering but that was it. He found himself in the middle of his father's expectations and his own incapacity to decide. There was one thing, though that he felt absolutely sure of. He wouldn't go to the US or anywhere else. Whatever major he decided, his college would be somewhere in Toronto.

Because Rose had planned to go there.

He didn't say this directly at first. It came up in conversations. Subtle implications that it would be nice to be in the same city for college. But when he told her truthfully, things started to go downhill.

Rose panicked.

College was a big deal. The fact that Dev had considered her in such an important decision made their relationship more significant than she had imagined.

She had also started noticing peculiar things. For a long while now, very few guys had shown any interest in her. Half their school assumed that Dev and Rose were already dating. The other half considered them to be so close that no one wanted to get into the middle of it. The problem was, they weren't entirely wrong.

Dev knew everything about her - moods, preferences and her wildest dreams. He knew how to make her happy and what made her sad. He almost never got upset with her. But when he did, on a rare occasion or two, she couldn't handle it. She'd lose sleep and appetite till he came to her again. This strange reliance on him, scared her. His equal reliance on her, terrified her.

Rose started to retreat. She grew distant from Dev and found opportunities to do things without him.

"Are you mad at me?" Dev asked her one day.

She'd been walking back from school alone when he approached to join her. "No." she replied, footsteps quickening. "Why do you ask?"

"You've been avoiding me. Have I done something?"

Rose focused her gaze on the street ahead, fingers closed around her books, clutching them tighter against her chest.

"Wait." he said, softly.

Her feet halted.

"We were supposed to meet at the library. And you cancelled last minute." He ran one hand through his hair. "You've been bailing out a lot. What's wrong, Ro? Tell me."

Instant regret grew inside her. She didn't want him to feel this way. "I don't know how to explain."

"Why?" Dev implored. "You can tell me anything. It's just me."

She swallowed painfully. The bags felt too heavy to carry.

Sensing an internal turmoil, Dev said, "Do you want to meet later? By the Oak?"

She nodded.

The field was empty as usual. The sun was still shining in all it's evening splendor. Dev was already there. He wore a dark blue denims and a gray t-shirt, one hand inside the pocket of his jeans, his back to her. She walked slowly finding the image ahead of her oddly mesmerizing. From afar, the tall, thin profile of a young boy stood as center point for the earth and skies; as a prelude to the massive oak tree ahead. When her steps echoed close by, he glanced sideways, giving her a soft smile.

She melted...instantly. Days of confusion and overwhelm seem less important. There was no one here but him. Amidst the green vastness, it felt easier and safer to talk to him.

"Why are you standing here?" she asked coming to a stop beside him. When had he grown so tall? She had to tip her head back meet his gaze.

"I was waiting for you."

The reply had been simple and unsurprising. He always did wait for her. But today, for a reason that she could not understand, the words took a more different shape. They covered the short trek to the tree in silence and sat under the refugee of the sprawling leaves, resting against it's thick solid trunk.

"Mom isn't feeling well again." She blurted.

"What happened?"

"I don't know! She won't tell me. And dad isn't saying anything either!" Days of frustration had made her exhausted and angry.

Dev put his arm around her, letting her head fall on his shoulder. "I'm sorry. I had no idea. My mom didn't tell me anything either."

"I don't think Auntie knows. So don't mention it yet. I think mom wants to have that conversation with her when she's ready." Her fingers fidgeted, nervously. "But there's something else. I can't keep things from you. It makes everything harder."

"So don't. Tell me, what's wrong. I'll fix it."

"That's just it. I don't want you to fix it."

He looked confused.

"I don't want you to fix things for me." She straightened and turned to face him. "I don't want you to keep doing things for me. I want you to do what you want!"

"But I want to do do things for you."

"You shouldn't!" Her voice grew loud, startling Dev.

"I'm sorry. I didn't mean to yell." she said, guiltily, biting her lower lip. "I just..." Words were hard to form when feelings grew so erratic. "College is important Dev. It's the first step we'll take towards building a career, our own lives, everything."

"Yes, I agree." his voice was soft, delicate, as if he were worried that anything he might say would makes things worse.

"I don't want to be the reason you feel distracted from prepping for college."

"Distracted?" Dev asked incredulously, "I am already distracted. You're helping me focus."

She waved one hand in dismissal. "Why don't you want to go to the States? Your dad expects it."

"I don't want to"

"Why not?"

He made a loud sound of frustration, exhaling a long, painful breath. "Why are pushing me to go away? Don't you want me to be around Toronto?"

"Yes, but only if you want to!" she yelled.

"I want to!" Dev's voice was losing its calm as well.

"No, you don't!" she continued. "The only reason you're even thinking of Toronto is because I'm planning to apply there. When we both know that the truth is, you want to try for Engineering school somewhere in the States."

They were standing now, facing each other. Both their faces flushed with anger. There was confusion, uncertainty and too many underlying emotions that they were too ill-equipped to comprehend.

"You're factoring me into your future plans." Rose accused.

"So?"

"So, what!" She threw him a look of disbelief. "You shouldn't. You need to figure out what you want out of your life. What you're good at. The person you want to be, Dev."

"And is it necessary that I must do this somewhere far away from you?"

But she was no longer listening. "You know how scared I feel sometimes thinking about it? If you make decisions based on me, and then you realize you don't like it, you'll hate me!" Her eyes pin balled on the ground from left to right. "And I'm starting to realize that half the school thinks we're dating."

"Why do you care what the school thinks?" An ache buried in his voice.

"It's our school. Our friends. And they're all thinking that we..." Her eyes shot upward boring into his with such intensity, it made him shook him a little inside. "We aren't dating, are we?"

The moment of silence felt longer than it was.

"No." Dev assured, quietly. "We aren't dating." The relief on her face was like a stab to his heart. He blinked and took a step ahead. Two fingers reached touched her cheek. The action was utterly soft and entirely too overwhelming. A sigh escaped her and she peered into him, letting him see every vulnerability.

The moment betrayed both - the question she had asked and the answer he had given her.

"I want you to remember something." he whispered. "Nothing will ever make me hate you, Ro. Nothing."

Chapter 11

Back then -

Dev's father made no effort to conceal his anger and disappointment. Anjee tried to intervene, but father and son matched each other in their stubbornness.

At the same time Cathy fell increasingly ill. She spent long days in her room with headaches that grew more and more frequent. Rose found out much later but her father's business had suffered terrible loses. For one reason or another, contracts were not being fulfilled on time.

Dev and Rose spent the last year of high school with an underlying sense of anxiety and despair.

One evening, weeks after her eighteenth birthday, the things really turned.

The annual spring carnival had arrived. It had been set up at the outskirts of the suburb on an open green master about a mile away from their oak tree. Every year Rose and Dev went together.

This year Dev went alone. Rose went with Miles Hutchinson.

The gossip around them had grown. Everywhere Rose went, it was assumed she was either meeting Dev or waiting for him. The boys in their class didn't go beyond friendly conversation no matter how many hints she dropped. Conversations with Dev had gotten strained. They spent most of their time either arguing or making up for some previous misunderstanding. Rose knew that for the large part she was responsible. Dev was trying his best to make her happy and do what she liked. But the more he did that, the more Rose realized how much he knew her and how little everybody else did.

In a moment of rash boldness, she asked Miles Hutchinson if he wanted to go to the spring fair together. He was a sophomore at college on a weekend visit to her parents' house.

Thirty minutes into the evening Rose realized that Miles hadn't quite understood her question or rather she hadn't made herself quite clear. Because he seemed to be content in believing that they were casually strolling the make-shift lanes of the carnival as nothing more than friends. At one point she found herself standing by herself.

"Where's Miles?" A voice accused in her ears with such suddenness she gasped in shock, one hand snapped to her chest.

"Dev!" she cried. "You scared me."

He frowned, crossing his arms over his chest. "Well?"

"Some of his old friends wanted to catch up with him. So..." her voice trailed, averting his gaze. "I haven't even tried Penny's new ice cream flavor yet."

Dev sighed, feeling his irritation seep away at the sight of her innocent pout. "I haven't either." he admitted, running one hand through his hair. "Let's go."

Miles Hutchinson was forgotten. Everyone else was forgotten. The spring fair felt brighter and more cheerful. Rose found herself immersed in pure happiness that came only with Dev. They played carnival games, rode the Ferris wheel and sampled odd flavors of chocolate from their favorite local ice cream maker. Rose dragged him toward a young photographer who took photos of them against the fabulous backdrop of the festivities.

It was well past midnight when they headed back home. He had his arm around her and she let her head rest on his shoulder. When Dev stood at the threshold of her front door, she pulled him in without hesitation. Her parents were out for the weekend. Another visit to another doctor in hopes of finding another treatment for the mother. Rose pushed those thoughts away as she ushered them into her bedroom and locked the door.

Rising on her tip toes, she kissed him. It was a touch, just a tentative nervous moment, as if she were measuring her own courage. When he took a step ahead, lowering his face to hers, she pressed her mouth again, this time in a strong, insistent kiss. His arms naturally came around her waist, pulling her flush against him. She held his shoulders dragging him, till the back of her knees hit the bed.

"Rose," he murmured, "are you sure?"

"Yes." she replied, plainly. "I'm sure."

"But we aren't dating. Are we?"

Her eyes fell and she shook her head automatically. "Do you want to..." the doubt slipped past her lips before she could stop herself.

His index finger curved under her chin, gently coaxing her to look up at him. Cupping her cheek in his palm, he sighed, "That you even have to ask..."

She sank on the bed, pulling him with her.

Rose had once stumbled upon an intriguing book in the library. She had blushed profusely as the pages turned. Though a lot of it sounded scary, a small passage had stayed with her. It said:

'The thing about first times is that there is so much emotion, so much fear and so much to discover that no matter how life turns thereafter, one never forgets it. The years roll by but the sensation of being touched, for the very first time, still lingers on the skin. The memory of holding and being held by another resurfaces on a quiet, unsuspecting evening. The thing about first times is that it creates a bond with one person. Even when the bond breaks, the memory forever remains.'

Afterward, they lay in bed finding comfort in the quietness, as their breaths evened.

"Do you regret it?" he whispered.

She turned her body sideways, reaching to drape one arm over his chest. He covered her hand with his.

"No." she said. The beat of his heart drummed softly under her palm. "I wanted you to be my first."

He pushed her hair away from her face and leaned in to kiss her again.

She smiled, truly happy in that moment. Her eyes memorized the hard ridges of his faces, the slop of his nose and the shape of his mouth. She blushed, at the thought of that mouth all over her skin only minutes ago.

The weeks that followed however didn't let the bliss continue. Cathy went into critical decline and had to be hospitalized. Dev's father had made the entire house a battle ground over his son's decision not to go to the States. Between a stressful home and the pressure for college applications, Rose and Dev struggled to balance their emotions.

It wasn't a single fight or any one specific reason. It was the cumulative effect of a series of small arguments and mistakes. They fought over every little thing, trivial words spoken in haste. Dev became overbearing. He questioned her more than needed and got angry when she preferred the company of other boys. Rose avoided him even when she really wanted to just be with him. They fell into a confusing, hurtful circle from which neither knew how to break free.

He found her sitting on a bench one day outside school. She wasn't alone. Their classmate and Dev's soccer teammate Ben was sitting next to her, his arm around her shoulder. Rage erupted inside Dev. He glowered at Rose and stormed off without saying a single word.

Later that evening she headed to the Oak Tree. They hadn't planned on meeting, nor had she told him that she was coming. But when she arrived, he was standing at his usual spot by the oak tree. She went to him quietly. He didn't turn...didn't move. With his head thrown back watching the mighty branches over them, he spoke,

"Do you want to tell me how you feel?"

"No..."

"Do you want to know how I feel?"

Her heart hurting badly, cracking deeper and deeper. "No."

He swallowed, controlling his own tears that threatened to follow.

Weeks later, during which they had completely stopped speaking to each other, Rose found out through friend that Dev had began to apply to schools in the States. She ran home crying all the way. Soon, it was time for their prom. By now the whole school had realized that Rose and Dev had 'broken up'. No one questioned when they both arrived solo, barely looked at one another and quietly left early.

Their mothers tried to intervene, but their children were too stubborn and too hurt to see any reason. The Malhotras were planning to move in the pursuit of expanding their business.

The end of high school felt like an innocent story had met a tragic end.

Rose had been accepted to Ryerson University for design but that no longer held happiness and excitement. The doctors had told her father that the chances of her mother's survival looked bleak. Dev was definitely going to the States. Her classmates began to leave for college.

One evening when she entered her mother's hospital room, she found Anjee Aunty sitting by her mother's bed, eyes glistening with emotion. Dev stood by the window, shoulders slumped, deep sadness on his face. Dev's little sister, Annie, who was thirteen at the time, was holding Cathy's hand, sitting on the other side of the bed, looking frightened.

Cathy looked small and fragile. She raised one shaking hand, a tube running from her wrist all the way to a machine at the back. Anjee reached to hold the weak hand and leaned forward. Cathy whispered, shallow words punctuated by coughs. Anjee nodded then placed one palm on her friend's forehead in a loving gesture. Whatever Anjee had replied seemed to have soothed Cathy because her face broke into a visible relief. She looked at Rose then at Dev, then back at Anjee, whispering a request.

"Come, beta." Anjee Aunty said to Rose, then gestured for Annie to leave with her. Dev began to follow but she shook her head. "You wait." she said to her son, then glanced at Rose. "Your mother wants to talk to both of you."

When the door closed behind them, Dev and Rose stood silently looking at each other. They hadn't spoken a single word in three months.

"My love..." her mother's voice wheezed from the bed. Rose took the stool on the right of her mother's bed. Dev sat on the other side. Cathy held out her hands towards them and they both moved simultaneously to gently clasp each palm.

"I know you're fighting." she wheezed so softly, both Rose and Dev had lean in close to her to listen. "I don't have enough time left to hear the whole story..."

"Mom don't say that." Rose cried. Dev squeezed Cathy's hand, feeling his insides crack with helplessness.

Cathy smiled at her daughter, sad yet peaceful. "It's alright, love. I've made peace with it. You're a wonderful daughter and" she coughed, "I have faith in you. You'll always have my blessing and my love."

Rose was weeping now, silent and resigned.

"Whatever it is you're fighting about, no matter how bad it may have gotten, it isn't worth it, children. It doesn't matter. Trust me. I'm standing at the edge and telling you the truth. It doesn't matter." She sighed, drawing in a breath with much effort. "Fight all you want but in the end, forgive each other. Life is fickle. One second it promises you eternity and in another it threatens to shut down completely. You cannot know which side on." Whatever strength she had in her, she used it to bring their hands close to her chest - the only form of embrace she could manage. "Dev," she glanced at the boy whose eyes were shone with hurt and fear. "Take care of her."

"Mom..." Rose tried to interject.

"Wait, darling. Let me say it. I'll die peacefully knowing that I did whatever I could." Cathy peered at Dev. "I can see it in your eyes. You don't have to say, my dear."

Dev exhaled. His eyes prickled and words failed to come out of his mouth. "Aunty..."

"Promise me." Cathy implored, a heavy cough leaving her body.

"I don't think I'm worthy of..."

"Promise me, Dev." Cathy repeating, her voice now carrying a command, urgency and desperation. "Promise me you'll look after her."

"Mom, please, don't ask him that." Rose tried to interject once again but Cathy was staring intently at Dev.

"What if she doesn't want me to?" Dev whispered, weakly.

"I know what she wants. And that is why I'm asking you this. You both can fight as much as you like. Make mistakes, learn and move on. Build your lives whichever way you like. But I need to know, at the final stretch, towards the end, before the finish line, you'll be there for her...you'll look after her. Promise me, Dev."

Dev stared into the older woman's eyes, letting her see the full force of his feelings. It was ironic that she should be the first one to see it. Or perhaps it wasn't ironic at all because what she saw in his eyes in those moments was the answer to her dying wish.

His head moved slowly, a tear rolling past his cheek. "I promise."

Four days later Catherine Barnes died.

Chapter 12

Back then -

For months Rose had been living with the horrifying possibility of losing her mother but now that it had really come to be, she fell apart. It seemed like her tears would never end. Her grief grew unsurmountable.

On the day of her mother's funeral Rose stood by her father. He had put up a brave front but they both knew he was broken inside. Her own sense of comprehension was lost. She wasn't aware of the proceedings around her. She wasn't aware of the people who gave their heartfelt condolences and sympathetic hugs. She wasn't aware that throughout the ceremony quiet tears fell from her eyes.

And she wasn't aware that Dev had one arm around her the whole time. He hadn't left her side for a moment.

He tried his best to talk to her. He apologized, more than once. But Rose had sunk into a shell and Dev was slowly running out of time. He had to head to California any day now.

"You should go." Rose said two weeks before he classes were to begin.

He hadn't even started packing. "I can't leave you here like this."

"I'm going to leave soon, too."

"No, you aren't. I know you deferred the semester."

Rose sighed, too exhausted to deny the truth.

"Rose, listen to me." They were sitting in her living room. Dev fell to his knees in front of her, bringing his face to her eye level. "I know this is hard but think again. Do you really want to defer? Maybe starting college now is what you need."

"I won't leave my dad here like this."

"Like what? Rose you cannot help him by stalling college."

"I won't go."

Dev's heart sank. He moved to sit cross legged, burying his face in his hands. For a long while they remained silent.

"There's no point, waiting. Go, Dev."

"Why are you doing this?"

"I'm doing nothing!" Her voice broke, anger surging into those blue eyes. "That's the problem. There's nothing I have been able to do. I watched for months, watched my own mother slip away and now she's gone. All I could do was nothing! And you and I..." She fell sideways, resting her head on a cushion, her body curling into a small space.

"I'll defer too." He muttered, shaking his head. "I'll wait for you to feel better."

"Please, Dev." She whispered, staring into nothingness. "Just leave."

"Rose, I promised your mother..."

"It was wrong on her part to make you promise that. She wasn't thinking straight."

"You know that's not true."

She blinked, painfully. "What is left in that promise? She isn't here anymore. And I..." she choked. "I don't want your help." Her mind was spiraling out of control. "I can't force you to leave for college. But if you stay I won't speak to you. I won't meet you. There's nothing left between us."

His insides burned with agony. "Do you really believe that?"

"Yes." Her voice felt alien even to her own ears.

Dev could delay his departure by only one more week. And in that week he tried every waking minute to get Rose to change her mind. Every attempt failed. The days ended and just like that, he found himself on a plane headed to San Francisco.

But he didn't give up even then. He made innumerable attempts to reach her. Dev's calls were repeatedly ignored, texts unanswered and emails deleted. He even called her dad. Dan was sympathetic but couldn't succeed to change his daughter's mind. Dev understood that she was hurting but his own heart could only take so much.

He missed her and he hated being away from her.

He couldn't concentrate on school and struggled with classes in his very first semester. Rose somehow found out. In a last act of defiance, she sent him a text, 'I miss you too. But you're better off without me." Then she changed her phone number. It wasn't that he couldn't reach her after that. But the message was his breaking point. It wrenched his heart. He finally did the one thing he thought he would never do - he gave up.

For months that followed, Rose dreamed of the last time she saw him.

It was the evening before his flight. She was waiting at the same spot where he usually stood. She didn't glance at his approaching form. When he stood beside her, she said, her eyes focused at the setting sun, "I'm glad you're leaving."

"That makes one of us."

"It's the right thing to do."

"Is it?" He turned his body to face her. "Ro," he whispered, "look at me."

And just like that, she did.

"If I call you, will you answer?" he asked. The question was futile. He knew the answer. But he couldn't help himself.

"No."

"Will you call me?"

Her eyes stared into his. Tears fell past her cheek. She shook her head. Swallowing a giant lump in her throat, she croaked. "This is for the best. I wish you happiness. Goodbye Devraj Malhotra."

The finality made him angry. He had made up his mind to accept her goodbye but he suddenly felt the urge to get something more...anything more. With an abruptness that startled them both, he pushed her against the bark of tree, letting her back collide with solid wood. He slammed him hands flat against the trunk on either side of her, caging her with his body.

"Dev!" her eyes grew wide with alarm.

He closed the distance between them. Reaching to hold her cheek in his palm, he swiped the tears away with his thumb. When he leaned forward to kiss her, she turned her face. It felt like someone had punched him. His lips pressed against her cheek with a terrific desperation. For a long moment neither moved.

"If you ever need me," he whispered. "You only have to call."

Her chest rose and fell rapidly. If she'd said a single word, given him a single indication, he would've dropped everything and stayed. She knew that.

She said nothing. She watched as his body jerked away from her. She watched as he turned around and took three steps head. He pivoted one last time to face her. His cheeks were streaked with tears. Her knees weakened and sunk to the ground, transferring her weight onto the earth beneath.

She watched, in agonizing silence, as he turned around and walked away. ..away from her life.

Chapter 13

Present day -

I'm in Dev's apartment. Her mind echoed, early next morning. Yesterday, if someone had predicted that this is where she would wake up, Rose would've felt sympathetic to the madness.

And yet, here I am. In a bed which is right across the hall from his. She padded to the living room and found Dev on the couch, his feet resting on the coffee table ahead. The television screen on the wall in front of him played a Formula 1 race. He glanced over his shoulder and turned off the television.

"Don't mind me. You can watch the..."

"I wasn't really paying attention." He looked calmer and more like his usual controlled self. "Coffee?" He was already headed to the kitchen before she could say yes.

Rose sank on the couch, reclining sideways, watching him. He was in his pajamas - loose sweatpants and a relaxed printed t-shirt. His hair was tousled, thick locks grazing his forehead. Sunlight had filtered through the white curtains casting a line of glow across his cheek and a part of his hair..

Gone was the thin, lanky teenager. In it's place stood a man with smooth ridges of muscle, strong arms and broad, heavy shoulders. His body exuded strength, vitality, action and purpose.

The untouched honesty of your teenage years was still present on his face but now something else lurked beneath it; something a little dark and a little dangerous. Between the sharp angle of his jaw and the scatter of a dark stubble, his innate boyishness carried with itself a possibility of sudden, quiet conquest. As if, any moment now, he would break into a smile and wink, charming his way into the heart of every onlooker only to get inside and wield his power before they had to chance to recognize or stop him. They were left with no choice but surrender.

A restless sleep which broke at the crack of dawn, is what Dev could manage at best. But that was enough time for him to think and calm down. Handing her a cup of coffee, he took a seat on the arm chair.

"I'm sorry about last night." he said, quietly. When she looked astonished, he continued, "I shouldn't have yelled at you and said all those things. You already had too much going on and I..." He sighed, regretfully, pressing his lips.

Rose understood right then that he would forever be a contraction. Because even when he apologized, she felt like it was an insult; an insult to herself that he should have to apologize at all.

"I didn't want to take that job. It was my third evening and..." she shook her head, "It wasn't the right decision. I admit. I just got desperate."

"I shouldn't have blasted on you...not without knowing everything. I'm sorry."

"It's alright. A lot happened yesterday. Let's try to move on."

They sipped their coffees in silence. Rose took this time to send a message to Samantha saying that she was visiting a friend for a couple of days. It wasn't entirely false, after all.

"What am I going to do now?" she whispered, mostly to herself.

"We can get something to eat. There's a bunch of..."

"No, I mean, about my job."

"Oh." He thought for a moment. "We'll figure something out."

We?

"First, lets get changed and head out."

"But..."

"You can't plan anything on an empty stomach, can you?"

It was strange to shower in his bathroom and dress in his guest bedroom, all the while aware of his presence across the hall. It was strange to see him standing by the window, when she stepped into the living room; beads of water still clung to the ends of his freshly cleaned hair. He was on the phone, rapidly giving instructions while they put on their shoes and left the apartment.

"You look...nice." he said, guiding them towards his parking spot.

She looked down at the simple black denims and the printed off-white sweater. There wasn't anything remotely pretty about it.

"You always say that." she smiled, shaking her head. It was true.

"And you," he slipped into the driver's seat, "still don't believe me."

It was a gloomy morning to say the least. The trees, in contract however, were more vibrant and green, infusing the damp air with a subtle positivity. Rose found herself feeling skittish in the car. Twice, their shoulders bumped and twice something electric whirled inside her stomach. Finally, ashamed of her own childish behavior, she crossed her arms over her chest, sat back in the seat to the corner, as far from him, and his shoulder, as was possible in that confined space.

She wouldn't have been so hard on herself had she known that Dev was internally punching himself for being ridiculously affected by her perfume. He couldn't understand, for the life of him, why his male ego seemed to revel in the simple fact that she was sitting next to him in his car.

"You know, I thought we were just going to get brunch somewhere close." Rose quipped, once she realized that they were heading towards Downtown.

"We will. But it's about time you saw Vancouver."

"I have been around."

Dev chuckled, "I doubt it."

Despite the rain, Saturday morning brought out the joggers and runners on the street. Young families with little kids were out and about. Small local markets were set up in a couple of different blocks.

"There's a food truck down there." Dev pointed to a corner on a busy street. "It comes only Saturday mornings. Best donuts you'll ever have."

That was just the beginning. They walked to another small spot that served only tacos. A farmer's market on another street had a booth from a local bakery serving eclectic kinds of artisanal breads and cheeses. Another truck on a different corner apparently made the best Cajun fries. By lunch time they were already too full to sit down and eat a full meal so they continued exploring the city and sampling food.

They were idly walking by a street in Gastown when Dev got a video call. To her surprise, he answered promptly, while continuing to walk. Two male voices boomed from the phone at once.

"Who won?" Dev asked, impatiently.

"Verstaaaapan." a voice announced, dragging the name.

"Nice!"

"You missed a good race." The other voice spoke and Rose recognized that it belonged to Nash.

"Yeah, I know. I'll watch the highlights later." Dev replied.

She tried to be quiet and side step out of the frame but it was too late. Inadvertently she had appeared in the background of his video call. It was barely for a moment but his friends had noticed.

"Wow wow" the other voice exclaimed, "Malhotra, you got a girl with you?"

Dev grinned. Without hesitating, he turned the phone towards Rose. Startled, she tried to push it away but not before Nash asked, "Is that Rose?"

"Bring her on." the other voice said without waiting for a confirmation

Dev glanced at Rose and winked. She ignored the tiny flutter in her stomach and shook her head vigorously, silently mouthing no no no. He leaned forward to mute his video, and turn the phone camera a little to the side.

"It's just Roman and Nash"

"No!" she exclaimed, "I wouldn't know what to say."

"Just say hi." He added with a hint of mischief in his voice. "If you don't come now then they will assume something's up."

Taking her silent blush as a yes, Dev pulled her to a corner on the street and pointed the phone in front of them. If anything, she blushed harder because now his hand was gently placed on her back, bringing her close so they could both be visible in the video frame.

The screen was divided in two sections. On one side was Nash, looking tousled and clearly still in bed. The second section was covered by a young man with striking gray eyes and dressed in a blue button down shirt. She managed a tentative smile, waving her hand awkwardly.

"That's Roman" Dev introduced. "He's in London at the moment. And you know Nash, of course." He's in..." Squinting one eye, Dev tried to remember, "Paris?"

"Bern." Nash replied with a sheepish smile.

"What? When?"

"Just arrived."

Nash received a dramatic eye roll from both his friends.

"You must've already run out of pages on your damn passport. Which one are you on? Third? Fourth?" Dev asked with dry amusement.

Nash replied, mildly exasperated. "Just the second one."

"If you get on Instagram, Nash," Roman drawled, "you'd have a huge fan following just based on the number of places you check into, in a week."

"Nothing's going to make me get on your precious Instagram." Nash scoffed. "Besides, if I ever need a dose of popularity, I'll just make an appearance on your account. How many followers do you have now?"

"A few."

"A few hundred thousand, you mean?" Dev

"oh... ha ha." Roman chuckled, dryly. "Says the guy with a million followers."

"You have a million followers?" Rose asked him, alarmed.

"Don't misguide her." Dev frowned. "It's my company's account and there's a marketing team to manage it."

"So the shirtless pictures of the Malhotra heir sailing in the Chanel islands, is a marketing decision?" Roman smirked, pointedly.

"Shut up, Fitzgerald. If I start picking out your Instagram exploits, from your personal account, we'll be here all day. And what are you laughing about?" Dev asked pointedly to Nash, "The fact that you don't exist on social media is bigger proof that your life has more secrets than the world can handle."

"Anyway..." Nash hastened.

"Yes, anyway." Roman chimed, "We've been impolite boys, ignoring the pretty lady." The way Roman looked at her made her certain that he must've broken too many hearts in his relatively young life. "Ms. Rose, please don't mind us, we have a tendency to ramble on."

"Oh, no, that's quite alright." Rose said, feeling extremely self-conscious as three pairs of eyes focused on her. In her nervous haste, she blurted, "Sorry, I made Dev miss the Formula 1 this morning."

Only when the three unanimously chuckled, did she realize what her words actually implied.

"Did you, now?" Roman grinned, his eyes narrowed with amusement.

"Oh no, that's not what I mean." she said quickly. Biting her lower lip nervously, she felt a warm rush up her neck.

"Let her be, Roman." Dev's hand caressed her back in a motion that was meant to comfort but ended up making her more nervous. "She'll regret ever meeting my friends."

"Since we've established that you were at his place very early this morning," Nash stressed 'very early', "did he make his famous omelet for you?"

"Oh, the omelet..." Roman groaned with longing.

Rose shook her head, smiling a little. "I didn't know he had a special omelet."

Before Dev could interject, Roman began to explain, "For years we've tried to find out what's in that tiny glass jar. He sprinkles that—" He rubbed his index finger and thumb in a sprinkling motion, "— that damn powder and we cannot stop eating. At this point I'm going to say it's a new type of drug."

Rose grinned and glanced sideways at Dev. He ran one hand through his hair, a sheepish grin on his face, looking utterly boyish.

"We've tried all types of tactics" Roman continued, "Alcohol, drugs, threats, kidnapping —"

"Kidnapping?" Rose's eyes grew wide.

"— he has refused to divulge that secret."

"Junior year," Nash started with unnatural eagerness. "The weekend before finals..."

"Shut up, Nash." Dev rolled his eyes. "I was asleep, alright. That's why I didn't realize..."

"That we'd taken you at the hill top across the city?" Roman asked, cheekily. "What's it going to be then, Malhotra? Maybe your Rose here can convince you to tell your friends about the brown jar with the green lid."

Dev found that he liked that sound of his Rose a little too much.

"Green lid?" Rose asked, innocently. "You mean —"

"Don't say it!" Dev's hand circled upward to cover her mouth but not before the words tumbled out of her.

" — Anjee Aunty's masala?"

The moment she'd uttered the words she knew she had made a grave mistake. There was a resounding yelp from the phone and a loud, aggravating groan from Dev. His palm slapped across his eyes. The two boys swore and teased, basking in the triumph that a long kept secret had been so easily revealed.

Without the need for kidnapping.

Rose clapped her fingers to cover her mouth, shocked and apologetic.

"You bastard!" Roman swore. "It's your mother's secret."

"Self control, my ass." Nash scoffed. "After god knows how many shots of tequila, you didn't spill the beans because you didn't know in the first place."

"And here, I once told you that I would pay you a million to share your omelet recipe." Roman rested a hand on his torso nursing an apparent chest pain.

Dev frowned. "You handed me a hundred-dollar bill."

"It was an advance." he replied with utmost seriousness.

"I think we've had enough." Dev shook his head.

His friends chuckled and with quick departing words, the call ended.

"I'm so sorry!" Rose exclaimed the second Dev was offline.

He laughed softly

"I didn't realize it was a secret."

"They're just playing around. My omelet doesn't taste that great. When three sleep deprived college guys are stoned in the middle of the night, they'll eat anything." Dev looked at her intently, a solemn curiosity flashing in his eyes.

"What?" she asked, feeling self conscious.

"Nothing." He blinked, trying not to read too much in the fact that she had remembered something so insignificant.

It poured all day but even the dismal rain couldn't dampen Dev's enthusiasm. He engaged her in endless conversation and told her stories, some hilarious, others intriguing and a few so weirdly outrageous she was very doubtful that they were actually true.

"Of course, it's true." Dev rolled his eyes, indignantly. "Nash and I did put goal posts on those two rooftops." He pointed high above to the rooftops on two separate towers very far apart.

Rose laughed, open and free, her troubles all temporarily forgotten. Her eyes sparkled and slowly, she started to relax.

That was precisely his aim for the day. He knew that she needed a break. Not to mention that he wanted to make up for his outburst from last night. There was much to be discussed but first he wanted to help her relax. Then slowly, he would talk to her.

He delighted in her smiles and was absolutely thrilled when she began to talk and open up. Yet, he couldn't help but notice the differences in this new, more solemn Rose. Life hadn't been kind to her. The adventurous spirit had receded into a shell enclosed by reservation and insecurity. Her posture was guarded and her eyes were reluctant to meet his gaze. She hesitated often, spoke softer than needed and withdrew at the slightest instance. It was difficult to see her like this, wary and inhibited.

As evening progressed, Rose realized that the last time she had laughed this way was... with him. He'd been right about the city too. She had lived here for five months but it felt like she'd only arrived yesterday. But even though Vancouver was beyond delightful in its charms, it was no match for the very appealing phenomenon that was Dev Malhotra.

Chapter 14

"Good isn't it?" Dev cocked his head toward her.

"Very good." she grinned. "Reminds me of Penny's."

It was late in the night and they were lounging on the outdoor couch of his balcony, eating ice cream that he had purchased from a street market hours ago. After a long while, Dev spoke. "You don't need to go looking for a new job."

She glanced at him, surprised. "What do you mean?"

He set his empty bowl aside and turned his body sideways, one leg folded underneath while the other fell to the floor. His arm was draped on the headrest behind her shoulders. "I know of an open position that will be perfect for it."

She looked away. "I can't do that."

"Why?"

They were sitting close; the subdued lights from the night sky casting a nocturnal glow on the pair.

"I can't," she swallowed, "I won't take favors from you this way."

"But...I don't understand."

A defeated sigh left her lips.

"What is your plan then?" he prodded, pointedly. "To throw yourself into the first open job out there and be miserable in it?"

"I don't want to take some random position" Her voice thick with emotion. "In case you haven't noticed, I don't have options to pick and choose from."

"But you do! I'm giving you an option, a much better one."

"I can't take your help." Her head shook back and forth.

"Why?" He was perplexed. "You were willing to take Sherman's help."

"That's different."

"Explain to me, how?"

"He's a professional acquaintance. And I asked him for a reference."

"I'm also giving you a reference."

"You're handing me the job!"

"And that's worse, because?"

"Because..." she started, searching for words to name her confusing emotions. "It just is, alright. It's different with you."

His lips pressed together fighting a scowl.

"I don't know how to explain." She set her bowl aside. "So much has happened in these past years. It's complicated and messed up."

"You're going to have to figure out a way to explain this." he crossed his arms over his chest, "because I'm not going to let it go."

In her mind, she'd always imagined what it would be like to see him again, talk to him. But now that he was right in front her, urging her to talk, her thoughts no longer made sense. Where would she begin?

"I'm in a lot of debt." The words tumbled out.

She rose from the couch and walked toward the glass railing. Placing her elbows on the metal edge, she leaned. It was easier to talk without looking at him.

"Mom's treatments and hospital bills took a toll on the finances. The doctors were trying many procedures and drugs. Insurance companies covered only partial bills. We had to pay out of pocket, for a lot of them. Mom was distraught even thought dad did his best to reassure her. Towards the end, when she knew that...that was it, I think a part of her was relieved that she would no longer be a burden." Her breath hiked. There was a shuffle behind her. "No, Dev. Please. Don't." Her voice wavered but she felt his movements halting. "Let me say this. It's been years and I think I finally should say these words out loud. For my own sake."

She took a breath, swallowing hard, and continued.

"When mom passed away so did our good fortune, I think. Dad had loses, huge problems with the company. My college fund, which was already quite small by then, had to be used to make up for those loses. Dad had to sell the house and move to a rental. Can you imagine what that must've been for him? Do you remember how much pride he had in his house? But it had to go. I extended my college deferment to by another semester. Dad was so upset. But I couldn't simply leave him to fight alone. I took up jobs, thinking it would be help. It did not. Finally, at the end of the deferment, even I had realized that it hadn't been the right choice. So I ended up taking a student loan and left for college." she paused, the memories and the guilt rushing into her heart.

"That's when my own failures begin. See, until then things not everything was in my control. It could be excused as bad luck. But doing well at college was my responsibility. And I didn't." she blinked, her eyes stinging, "I didn't do well."

She took a shaky breath. "I switched between majors a lot and took the wrong classes, thinking I could figure a way out to save dad's company. When I did badly in almost all those courses, I gave up on that goal and did what I should've done right in the beginning - design school. It was the only thing I'd ever been good at. But my previous mistakes cost me a lot time and a ridiculous amount of money. To compensate I was working forty hours a week and taking full time courses. I couldn't concentrate and barely managed to get passing grades. But passing grades don't get you good jobs. I took up whatever came my way... average jobs, nothing stable.

"Last year, I met a lady who was starting her own interior design firm in Vancouver and was looking to assemble her team. She was fantastic, really and even paid for my moving expenses. But by the time I arrived, some huge family issue led her to postpone her plans. I considered going back home but what was left for me there - no job, no references, a weak resume and a father who would suffer to see me struggle. So I decided to stay and went around looking for work. The only ones I could find quickly were sales positions at furniture stores. I met Matt Sherman at one of my shifts. For some reason he was impressed by me and offered me a job. He told me outright that it was only a three-month position. But it was the closest I had come to doing what I actually wanted. The three months passed in a flash however and nothing had worked out. I got another part time position at a sales company but I was running behind on rent and my interest alone is staggering. I was getting desperate so I asked Sam to get me a few shifts at the lounge. And... well, you know how that turned out."

When she blinked, her eyelids felt too heavy. A defeated sigh left her lips. "There you have it. Now that I've finally said it out loud, it doesn't seem all that complicated after all. Just eight years of failures rolled into a snowball effect that finally brought me here.

You want to know why I can't take your help? Because the prospect makes me feel intensely guilty. I haven't forgotten even a single detail of what happened between us. Of course, I remember. I was selfish and cruel. All those things I told you, they were so wrong, so mean, so hurtful. You didn't deserve it. Any of it. Do you think I've forgotten how many times you called in that first year after you moved? Even after I changed my phone number so carelessly? I remember every single text and every single email. I also remember how I ignored each one of them. And after ten months and seventeen days your texts and emails stopped. I had finally pushed you over the edge.

The years that followed were my own doing, a grave I slowly dug for myself. I swear, I didn't know you and your family had settled here. The last I'd heard, couple of years ago, your parents were thinking about Toronto or California. Had I known you were in Vancouver, I probably wouldn't have even come. I'm not proud to admit that but it's the truth. After everything I did, I couldn't find the courage to ever face you again. To be honest, I still can't.

To come here now, step into your beautiful life, that I am so happy you've made for yourself, and demand that you clean up my mess for me... I can't do it. I've made mistakes but I still have my sense of morality. It's just not right."

A strange calm flowed through her. This is how people must feel after confessing their sins. Her eyelids dropped close. She took a soft inhale then an exhale, concentrating on these two simple tasks. The sound of the traffic slowly ebbed as the city retreated into the night.

When a warm hand touched the small of her back, her eyes opened. She looked up sideways. His face was grave and unreadable.

Without a word, indication or even a pause, he turned her body toward him and held her face in his hands. His head dipped lower to press his lips against her forehead. It was a kiss meant to heal. Her eyelids dropped. Numbness travelled through her body. She was aware of only the tiny spot of heat on her forehead where his lips remained for many long moments. He drew back then pulled her close, enveloping her in his arms; unmoving, silent, just holding her, very tightly.

She broke.

Violent sobs tore from her body. Hot stinging tears fell freely as she cried. Her arms rose to his back, clutching at him with sudden, staggering desperation. She fell into him, burying herself into his chest, drowning into the warmth of his body. Strong, capable arms held her with a force so powerful, she'd never felt this protected in a very long time.

He held her effortlessly, absorbing her shudders and sobs, allowing the long restrained tears to wash away. He would hold her as long as she needed him to.

He would hold her like this forever.

"I miss mom." she confessed between the sobs. She didn't know what had made her say it.

One of his hands reached to curve over the back of her head, pressing her closer still.

"She'd be so proud." he whispered, his voice hoarse with emotion.

"Of what..." Rose let out a strangled sound between a sob, "What a failure I have become!"

"No." His replied, resolute. "She'd be proud of everything you've survived, on your own. She'd be proud of how strong you've grown."

When her breathing began to even, they settled back on the couch. He wrapped one arm around her shoulder, positioning her so she was tucked into his side. So warm and comfortable he was, that she would've easily drifted into slumber. But there was still something left to be said.

"I've tried to imagine how it would be if I ever met you again." She peered up at his face. "How I would say it? I owe you an apology, Dev. A very big one."

"You don't have to say that now." He stroked her back, softly with more affection than he thought he was capable of. She already worn out, he could see it in her eyes.

But she pulled away and sat up. "I want to. Now is as good a time as any." Her hands came to rest on her knees, head bowed and eyes downcast.

"I'm sorry, Dev." she sobbed. "I'm sorry for hurting you. I'm sorry for saying all those things. I'm sorry for forcing you to leave in that hurtful way. I'm sorry for all those times you tried come close and I pushed you away. Again and again. I had these expectations of achieving something grand. I didn't value what I had right in front of me. And then mom left. I was angry at the things around me, I was confused about what I really wanted and I took it out all on you. It's no excuse of course. And I take full responsibility for hurting you."

Dev's gaze softened. There was a part of him that had always waited for an apology but now that he had received it, he realized that it hurt, terribly, to see her like this.

He hadn't been waiting for her apology. He's been simply waiting for her.

A rush of protectiveness flowed through him. With an index finger, he gently raised her chin, coaxing her to look at him. Bright, electric blue eyes were filled with regret. So innocent, open and honest. He wanted to close the distance between them and kiss her, soft and slow. Maybe that would take the sadness away.

"You aren't responsible alone. I made mistakes too."

"You didn't!" she implored, brows furrowing "You gave me so much..." Her throat hurt. "so much...kindness. And I walked away from it without a second thought."

"But I gave you no freedom to be yourself. I was lost and in need for direction. So I expected you to be my constant inspiration. But what you really needed was to feel human. You needed the freedom to charter your own path."

"And what a fine job I've done of that." A humorless chuckle escaped her.

"That's not what I mean. I had no sense of self, no confidence in my own abilities. So I depended on you to fulfill that. But self worth is not something that can be borrowed. It has grow inside a person."

"Well, it's my turn now to lose my sense of self."

"No, Rose." He shook his head firmly. "You've had bad circumstances and you did what you had to, to survive them."

"That's not important." She mumbled, hurriedly, desperation in her eyes "Will you forgive me? Please, Dev?"

Tears had streaked her cheeks, the tip of her nose was red and strands of hair were in a loose disarray. She's so beautiful, he thought. There was a raw purity about her, an open honesty that went straight to his chest. He sighed. She needed to hear the words and so he gave them to her. "Yes, Rose. I forgive you."

Her eyes dropped and shoulders fell, as if something very heavy had been lifted off them.

"Come here." He extended an arm and drew her closer so she could rest her head on his chest. She hugged him, clinging to him sideways, letting the beat of his heart infuse a sense of peace into her.

"Dev." she whispered.

"Yes?"

"I've missed you."

He dipped his face lower, cheek grazing the side of her forehead. With two fingers, he pushed stray locks of hair away from her face, tucking it behind her ear.

"I've missed you so much." she repeated.

His chest tightened. So simply she had uttered the words. Without hesitation. He wanted to do the same. He wanted to tell her that every day for eight years, she had been a perennial thought in his mind, pushed back, in a safe secure corner of his consciousness, while he worked and lived and breathed. He'd dated a few women but it had never amounted to anything. Now, having her in his arms, he realized it was because, at some level, in some way, he had looked for her in every one of them.

But he didn't say those words. He couldn't find the courage or the will. The last time he had stepped over the line, it had destabilized his whole life. So instead, he whispered into her ear, "I missed you too, Ro."

The air blew softly, fluid and calm. The sky was illuminated by tiny bright stars. For a long time, they rested underneath the vastness of the open sky.

Slowly, as the city began to sleep and the stars continued to twinkle, the years behind them began to fade away in a manner that sand get washed by a single long sweep of a clear ocean wave.

Chapter 15

R ose finally relented.

"I'm only getting you to the door." Dev implored, the next day. "You are the one who has to do the work."

"Do you know how many people are desperate just to get to Simon Banfield's door?"

His face was hard and determined. "And I can tell you, with absolute certainty, that none of them would have thought twice about accepting my reference."

They were eating take-out pasta at his place. With her fork, she idly pushed the pasta from side to side.

"Look, everyone, and I mean everyone, needs help. Recommendations, references, putting in a good word - call it anything you want. It's all the same. We all need it in some way or another."

"But it isn't fair." Her elbows rested on the table and she buried her face between her palms. A long exhale followed. "I should've been able to do this on my own."

"No one can do everything on their own, Ro. Look at me. I have done nothing by myself. More than half the opportunities and privileges I get are because of my family."

"That's not the same. You're so good at what you do and that's helping your father's business."

"Exactly." Dev insisted, firmly. "This isn't the time for you to bring some misguided sense of morality. Turning down an opportunity like this isn't righteousness. It's stupidity. Don't look at me like that." His lips curved in half a smile when her face was scrunched in a wounded look. He took another bite then continued, this time with a little more tact. "Banfield doesn't take kindly to recommendations in the first place. He's made an exception for me. I showed him your work at Sherman's and based on that he's willing to give you a four-week probationary trial. In fact, since you're going there on my recommendation, he'll have a closer eye on you. Forget being bad the job, if you slack even moderately, you'll be out the door within a day. Not to mention I'll get an angry phone call. Whatever you do in that office, Rose, it'll all be on you. I will not, and cannot, help you do your job. But," his voice was solemn with a hard, pained undertone. "I will give you a push if I can. I think I can do that much at the very least."

An erratic rhythm set in her heart. She swallowed a lump, his words slowly taking root in her mind. "I won't slack." She murmured. "You won't get an angry phone. Not on my account."

"I know." He gazed at her, long and unblinking.

Rose barely got a day to make herself believe that she now had an unbelievable job prospect when Dev decided to spring another pivotal change.

He had refused to let her go back to her apartment. Only once he drove her back to pick up some more stuff. Samantha had stared at Dev the whole time. Partly marveling at the fact that the rude man from that awful night was actually a nice person, and partly disbelieving that Rose was actually friends with someone who was so out of their leagues. To Rose's utter astonishment, Dev invited Samantha to join Rose and stay at his apartment.

"It's really not a problem. You're her roommate." Dev explained, politely. "It'll only be for a few days. Till you both move into a new apartment."

Samantha's mouth hung open, completely off guard.

"What new apartment?" Samantha whispered hurriedly to Rose.

"I have no idea."

Samantha thanked him profusely but turned down his offer.

"I think Samantha wasn't comfortable with me." Dev remarked on their way back. "Maybe you can talk to her again and make her feel more welcome."

"I'll ask." Rose nodded. "But I think she was being honest. We've been living there for five months, you know. Ideally, I should also be there..."

"No!"

She sighed, ignoring the ball of warmth rolling in her stomach.

Back at his apartment which already felt familiar within a short span of a few days, he came from his bedroom holding a laptop in his hands.

"What do you think about this?" He settled on the couch beside her and turned the screen so she could have a look.

A series of photographs of a very elegant two-bedroom apartment were displayed on the screen. "Oh nice. Is it from one of the projects you're working on?"

"Not really." He shot her a meaningful glance.

It took her moment to understand. She retreated from the laptop as she'd been stung.

"No." She shook her head, alarmed.

"Yes." There was a mischievous twinkle in his eye.

"Dev, no."

"Rose, yes."

"I can't!"

"Yes, you can."

"I can't afford it."

"But I haven't even told you the rent yet!"

"You don't need to." she said. "I know the area and I know the rent that is demanded here. I'm sure, one hundred percent, that I cannot afford this even with a roommate."

"Hear me out," he began filtering details from his screen. "It's about fifteen minutes from here. The metro station is right behind it. Banfield's office will be about twenty, maybe thirty minutes by train. It's a great location."

"It doesn't matter! It's not in my budget."

He grumbled audibly, crossing his arms over his chest. His face was scrunched up in pure irritation. Part of her wanted to laugh at the brattish behavior. That is, until he announced arrogantly, "I'm not going to let you go back to that mouse-house."

Her eyebrows rose high on her forehead. "Mouse what?"

"Oh," he amended, mockingly, "would you prefer mole-hole?"

She tried to maintain a glare on her face. It was proving to be hard. "I would prefer you not making stupid rhymes about the place where I live."

"Where you 'used' to live." He patronized, lifting his fingers to make air quotes.

Annoyed, she leaned forward to push his hands away. He broke into a chuckle, further aggravating her. Her small hands smacked at his chest, trying to shove him. He didn't budge an inch of course. Instead, his fingers circled around her slender forearm and yanked her close, flush against his chest. The movement had been so swift, it made her gasp. His gaze locked with hers.

They'd been this close before, even more intimate. But that intimacy was shared between two teenagers who were barely deciphering their own feelings. They weren't teenagers now. And that fact didn't escape either of them. She'd been attracted to an eighteen-year-old boy. Now, at twenty-six, this man terrified her.

"Say yes." he ordered gently with an undertone that didn't leave room for opposition.

"Yes."

"The owner bought this apartment a long time ago. So I can negotiate on rent."

It occurred to her only then that he had told her to say yes to the apartment.

He continued, "Ask Samantha to live with you. Discuss with her and then tell me what total amount you can pay and I'll try to bring down the price as close to it as possible."

"Okay." her voice meek and barely audible. "Dev?"

"Hmm..."

"When I asked you if this was one of your projects, you said no. Was it because you don't need to work on it?"

He averted her gaze but before she saw a slow smile on his face.

"You already own it." she accused.

"I don't." he replied, casually. Then he glanced sideways and winked. "My father does. It is one of his investment condos. He bought it during pre-construction years ago. So the firm can afford to rent it out at a much cheaper price without making a direct loss."

"But you don't profit by giving it to me for a lower rent."

"I don't want to take rent from you at all."

"Dev." It was meant to be reproachful but came out sounded intimate.

"You haven't outgrown your stubbornness. It's gotten worse to be honest." He rolled his eyes, letting go of her arm. "We can set a rent amount that doesn't cause the firm to lose money."

"How will you explain it to your father? Won't he feel cheated."

"No one is getting cheated. I'm simply facilitating the transaction to satisfy both parties. Besides, my father will hardly notice, as long as the graph isn't in the negative direction."

There was an anxious apprehension on her face. "You're doing so much for me. How will I ever repay you?"

He blinked, staring at her with wonderment. He wanted to make her understand how little he was doing for her. How much more he wanted to do and how much more he thought she deserved. Her apprehension was naive and unfounded; it intrigued him. Ever since they were kids, he'd always believed that she was his responsibility...that it was natural, unquestionable to protect her. Why was she worried about repayment? Why did she question it at all? He was meant to look out for her. He was always meant to care for her...forever. "There's nothing to repay. It's just me, Ro."

Chapter 16

S imon Banfield was brand in himself, but the kind that justifies its flamboyance with a singularly superior skill. Rose had learned more in the twelve weeks working as a Junior designer than she had in the past eight years. To work directly with Banfield was an impossible feat. Even Dev's recommendation couldn't get her that. She was apprenticing under Banfield's Principal Designer, Cary Trussardi who turned out to be a brilliant mentor. Impressed with Rose's creativity and dedication, Cary had allowed her to attend a meeting with Banfield. In the confines of their office, this was considered a huge achievement. No assistant had been given that honor so fast.

Outside of work Rose found herself falling in love with design once again. A dam had been broken, giving way to a flood of creativity. She spent long hours at the office and at home, voluntarily pouring over books and catalogs creating multiple mood boards and developing aesthetics. Her evenings after work and weekends belonged to Dev. They were spending all their free time together.

For someone who appeared charming, carefree and relaxed, Dev was a work machine. His capacity to focus and put in the hours, was astonishing. When he'd callously told her that everything he had achieved was because of his family, he was being phenomenally modest. Dev was more invested in the details of every project than any other employee in his entire office. Contractors, flooring vendors, paint suppliers, property lawyers - just about anyone involved, Dev spoke to them regularly. His assistants were always on the edge, anxious that their boss would inevitably catch even the tiniest detail that they might've accidentally let slip by.

So many evenings they had dinner together at his apartment. Afterwards he'd drop her home which was only fifteen minutes away. If it was too late, she'd simply stayed over in his guest bedroom.

Occasionally, he had informal house parties. Friends, colleagues, acquaintances from out of town and anyone new who wanted to network in his expanded social circle, showed up for a couple of drinks on the weekends. Rose had an unspoken and open invitation to all his parties. In fact, at this point, his whole apartment was open for her to walk into at any time.

One Saturday evening, at one such informal get-together, Rose happened to overhear a conversation that piqued her interest. Alana Briggs, an interior designer who had recently opened her small firm was in conversation with a fashionably dressed young woman. Rose had met Briggs once before. The latter was in her mid-thirties with commendable experience and already had a long-wait list. The other young woman was discussing with Briggs, an apartment she had just purchased and needed someone to do the interiors. The woman, Jenny, had a small budget since it was her first home. Rose wasn't sure what possessed her to throw herself into their discussion. She managed to get Jenny on as client and proceeded to enjoy a very engaging conversation with the two women.

For rest of the evening, she tried her best to avoid looking at Dev because she knew that he had witnessed the entire exchange.

When the guests had left and it was just the two of them he said, without delay, "So you got yourself a little side hustle?"

Rose blushed, biting back a grin.

"But come now, Ro." He drawled, chiding her mockingly, "This was my party and my guests so isn't it 'unfair' that you get to take advantage of it." He air quoted the word unfair.

He was teasing her, she knew. There was a patronizing smirk on his face. That is why she only smiled, fighting a blush, and said softly, "But it was her whole apartment...in West Vancouver. I really wanted to design to be able to design it."

They had been sitting on the couch in his balcony. His arm was draped over the headrest portion behind her shoulders. He gave her a sideways glance. There was an amused intensity in his eyes. He dropped his hand and ruffled her hair, "Good girl. You're learning."

At any given day, Simon Banfield had a considerable stack of invitations to the best parties around the Vancouver area. His principal designers were invited too, who in turn selected a few members from their team to accompany them. It was opportunity for junior designers to meet serious peers in their profession and form good connections.

Since her very first week, Rose had accompanied Cary to every social event. At first she'd been apprehensive and awkward. But slowly, she started finding comfort with other designers from different firms. Faces had become familiar and conversation flew with ease. She spoke passionately about her work and learnt so much more about interior design, architecture, even the art of good conversation and power dressing.

She was heading to one such cocktail party that evening with her colleagues.

In a true Vancouver fashion, it also took place on a rooftop which was buzzing with enthusiasm. It had been a particularly positive quarter for real estate as a whole. People were buying houses more than ever before. Either that or current home owners were eager to spend on home renovations.

Rose stood in conversation with Mara Henderson, a style assistant at another prominent interior design firm. Mara had become a good friend and was currently discussing her last project which was a private home in Maple Ridge.

"Flute paneling is all the rage now. We're putting it everywhere - living room, bathroom, home office. Honestly, I'm all for it. This house I'm telling you about, we did flutes in matt black in the bathroom and small mirrors for the double sink. Very chic. Match with that matt black faucets and..." her gaze drifted to a spot behind Rose. "Oh, well well. They party just got a lot of more fun."

Rose turned to follow Mara's line of sight.

"Dev Malhotra." Mara stated with an amused smirk.

Rose felt like his name had been announced over a speaker.

Dev Malhotra entered the party alone but the eager reception he received from the host, who rushed to meet him, made it seem like he was the guest of honor for whom the entire party had been waiting for.

"What do you mean, a lot more fun?" she asked.

Mara laughed. "So you've met him before."

Rose startled, feeling a blush creep in. "Not sure what you mean..."

"Sweetie, you first question, if you wanted to sound this confident, should've been - who is he? Not, why is the party fun now."

She bit her lip, embarrassed.

"Relax. Every available, single woman here has crushed on him, at some point." Mara assured her, smugly.

Oh, Mara, you don't know the half of it, Rose sighed internally.

Dev Malhotra didn't just appear to be a good looking man, though he was exceedingly handsome, too handsome for women to handle. But he also brought with himself his magnificent personality and the compelling force of his name.

From the moment he entered, he wasn't left alone even for a second. He would be talking with few people in one corner, then someone would cut in either to join that circle or whisk him away. Often the host escorted a guest who was eager to get an introduction with the famous heir of Mulgrave Properties.

The full force of his personality was on display here. She knew he had gained success but this... this was too much. He was a mountain and she felt like a tiny mouse compared to it. Her conversations with other people had changed as well. Almost everyone made some mention of him.

Rose made no attempt to meet him.

She was heading to the far end of the large terrace when Simon Banfield stopped her.

"Rose." he said.

She was startled. Her exchanges with Simon had been limited to a few sentences. She didn't even realize that he remembered her name.

"Oh hello Si... I mean Mr. Banfield" she stuttered, feeling silly that she was getting nervous over a simple greeting.

"Simon will do." Banfield smiled. "Are you enjoying the party?"

"Yes, absolutely. I was just talking to Michael Stokes. He wants to discuss upgrading his Chilliwack farmhouse. I've set up an appointment for him on Tuesday with Cary. I'll send her a message about it."

"Good. But continue this one Monday." He paused for moment, accessing her. "I don't expect you to only work here, you know."

"Oh, of course. I'm having a wonderful time. Thank you for letting me come."

"My dear," Simon chuckled. "Half the people here wonder if I'm really a monster to my staff. One look at you and they're doubts will be proven true."

Rose smiled, sheepishly. "I just thought since I'm here, I could talk to a few more people..."

Simon was looking at her intently, his eyebrow raised with some sense of surety. Perhaps age or experience or both had given him this ability to be perceptive.

The words in her heart came pouring out. "I want to succeed at this so badly. I simply cannot screw, I mean mess this up. I've..." she shook her head and smiled nervously. "I cannot bear the thought of going backwards at all."

Simon nodded in understanding. A rare expression of kindness crossed his face. He spoke quietly. "I've been in the business a long time now so when I say this, take my words as gospel. You've walked into the office each day, earlier than most people, with a rare determination. The work you put in, shows result. As long as you do that each day, every day, you will not fail."

A gentle smile appearing on her face. After so many inconsequential jobs, an appreciate like this, from someone so senior, was a very big deal. Before her eyes began to feel a little hazy with emotion right in the middle of a party, she looked away and tried to cover her embarrassment with a meek thank you.

"You don't need to walk around with the weight of the world on your shoulders. Enjoy the party, really enjoy it. Make some friends without trying to set up professional appointments. Well," he paused, light amusement on his face. "if you find a good young man for a different, more informal appointment, then that's up to you."

She blushed, surprised Simon was actually making a joke.

"Go on," he patted her shoulder with paternal affection. "I've asked Wade to wait with a car downstairs. He will make sure you, Evelyn and Tim get home safely. Get a drink or two and have fun."

People became louder and more informal as the hour ticked. Rose had still not made an attempt to meet Dev. Maybe after the party she would go and say hi or just mention it to me sometime later at his apartment, when it was just the two of them. For now, though, it confused her to be in the same room as him and not approach him. Was it relief or disappointment? All these people here, they saw the charming, genius son of a property builder, the one who'd not only carry the torch to his family business but the one who was expected to double, even triple, the family fortune.

They were not wrong. But that's all they knew.

She had seen the part of him that no one here had access to. Early mornings, he'd walk into his kitchen, yawning lazily, in his faded pajamas, his hair tousled without a care. Quietly he'd make coffee and put bread in the toaster. Sometimes, she would enter his apartment in the evenings to find him in the middle of an intense video call, shirt sleeves folded over his forearms, tie discarded and his face frowning in disapproval.

All these people knew Dev Malhotra. None of them knew Dev.

She was standing around a round table now, with her colleagues and trying to partake in the conversation as best as possible. But every once in a while, more often than she'd like to admit to herself, her eyes drifted in pursuit of tall figure with black hair and brown eyes. He wore a black suit today, white shirt and no tie. The top button of his shirt was undone making the base of his throat appear irresistible.

A waiter brought a fresh tray of drinks for the table and someone decided to raise a toast. She barely heard his off-track sentence before raising her glass and emptying the contents.

Her phone buzzed.

It was a text.

From Dev.

"That was your fourth glass. How are you getting home?"

Chapter 17

Rose's heart had stopped beating. A shiver ran from her neck to her fingertips and right down to her toes. With shaky hands, she slipped her phone back in her small handbag.

With precise movements, she picked up another glass from the tray. Slowly, without pulling attention, she retreated from the group and walked to the edge of the terrace. The sparkling city lights blurred in her vision. She took a slow, meaningful breath. Inhale. A moment. Exhale. Another sip of the drink.

It wasn't important what drink it was, as long as she continued to bring it to her lips and swallow the liquid. Her feet hurt, despite the sensible height of heels. She leaned on the railing in an attempt to take some pressure of her toes.

"Oh Dev, so nice of you to join." A voice echoed behind, making her jump. Her heart palpitated and palms felt clammy. "You've finally graced us with your presence." Someone was teasing. There was chuckling and laughter and some more words.

She was aware that he was standing only steps away. How long had passed, she did not know, but at some point, the smell of his perfume was closer.

Ever so lightly, something warm touched a patch of her lower back. A hand reached for the glass that was raised halfway, lowering it a few inches.

"Tell me first," he whispered into her ear, "Then drink."

He was too close for comfort. The solid muscle of his chest was pressed against her left shoulder blade; the fabric of his jacket was rough against the length of her arm, but in the most appealing way possible.

When the words came out, her voice seemed unlike her own, breathless and weak. "Dan's asked Wade from the office to drop us home."

"Good." His hand left the glass and rested on the smooth metal railing. Her eyes fell on the long, hard line of his fingers, somehow looking more manly with the heavy smart watch around his wrist.

"Are you cold?" he whispered with genuine concern.

Her mouth had gone dry. She shook her head, softly.

He touched her elbow then trailed his fingertips upward, caressing the length of her slender arm. Slow and deliberate touches, from her bicep to her forearm and back again. She thought it was an attempt to comfort but he knew it was a desperation to touch.

"By the way," he continued to whisper, "you look beautiful."

It was putting it mildly. He thought she looked stunning; a magnificent creature that did not belong to this party or this evening or this world. It belonged... only to him. He had been abnormally aware of her to the same, perhaps even greater degree than she had. The only difference being, he was better at sleuth than she was. It was the old skill after all. He had years of practice...years of watching from the corners and protecting her from a distance without her ever realizing.

Until now.

Every time he felt her gaze on him, a violent pleasure bolted through him. His masculine pride swelled with primal satisfaction.

She was wearing a green fitted dress. It was by no means, revealing or exceptional fashionable. But he thought it was phenomenal simply because she made it so. His mouth spoke expertly about concrete and plywood but his mind was consumed by the shape of her body draped in forest green. The smooth curve of her waist, the length of her legs, the way she held back her shoulders straight and confident. Once in a while, she would flip her hair back, in the middle of a conversation and smile or chuckle. He felt a pang of envy then, especially if the onlooker was a man.

He could see now, a scarlet blush glowing on her face. It drove him crazy. Tugging at her elbow, he turned her around to face him. He was practically holding her in his arms now, one hand gripping her waist, the other idly touching her arm.

"Rose?" he urged. Her gaze was fixated on his chest.

"Hmm." she whispered, distracted. Her fingers touched the shirt on his chest, curling then uncurling. The action was very subtle. But he noticed.

"Look at me." his voice soft with a hint of command.

Automatically, her face lifted. In an instant the fathomless blue of her eyes sucked him in, making him forget his initial train of thought.

"Why were you staring?" he asked a little more strongly than he had intended to.

Had she been a little more coherent and sober, she would've had a fitting retort to his hypocrisy but the alcohol mingled with the power of this man was distracting her beyond logic.

"I don't know." she mumbled.

The words came out so innocently, so quickly, without any effort to refute, that it caused his face to soften.

So handsome. she thought, looking up at him

When his lips grew into a visible grin she realized that she'd said it out loud.

He pushed her hair away from her face, grazing her forehead. The pads of his fingertips trailed along the side of her cheek, feeling the silky softness of her skin.

"You are cold." he frowned when he noticed goosebumps on the length of her arm. "Where's your coat?"

"In the car."

Frowning, he held the lapels of his blazer and began to slide it off shoulders. But before he could, her palm uncurled on his chest, pressed firmly, halting him. "Don't, people will notice."

Someone called out to them. She jumped backward before anyone could notice so it just appeared that the two of them had been talking something insignificant. A camera was pointed toward the group of people, who huddled together for a picture.

Dev pulled her to join the group and drew her closer to his side. He said something over the top of her head, a reply to a comment that was made. She didn't catch any part of the interaction except that when he laughed, the soft vibration from his chest sent ripples through the side of her arm. The people around were smiling and laughing, finding a unanimous pose for the photo.

She was looking up at him unaware that the photographer was waiting. He dipped his head lower, a glint of humor in his eyes.

"Sweetheart," he whispered. "Look ahead and smile."

The endearment was deliberate, meant only to tease. But the way it came out - low, deep and resonant - sent waves of electricity. She shivered. In the next moment, her head had turned and she had smiled appropriately for the photo.

The host appeared out of nowhere and pulled Dev away. Away from her. A pang of sadness overtook her. It was irrational to get this affected by his absence. She walked to the bar with the intention of getting a glass of water but ending up holding two glasses of wine.

"Last call" the bartender had said and there was no Dev there to stop it.

She finished the first glass in two long gulps, then picked up the second one and looked around her for colleagues. After a whole evening of standing on heels, walking was getting quite uncomfortable now. She couldn't find Tim or Evelyn anywhere. Only a few guests remained while the rest were the cleaning and serving crew.

"What's wrong?" he appeared, seemingly, from nowhere. "And this?" he pointed to the empty glass, with disapproval.

"So?" she said, petulantly. "It's my wish."

"It's your wish to be unable to stand properly?"

"What? I am st..." but she noticed that he was holding her up with one arm. "Oh."

He sighed and for some reason, that irked her.

"It's all your fault." she accused, pushing away from him. The moment she freed herself, the ground beneath began to move, making her stumble.

"Oh God," he groaned, one palm pressed at his forehead and the other arm catching her easily, "Just stop moving, will you?"

"It's your fault!" She repeated. Arms rose to cross over her chest but she couldn't quite manage to appear forbidding.

"How is it my fault?" He asked, guiding them past the exit. At this point, he wasn't even asking her. He was simply dragging her along.

"You don't get to just appear and disappear whenever you want!" she jabbed one finger at his chest.

"What does that even mean?" he muttered.

Grumbling, she threw her hands up. They were standing in front of the elevator. Suddenly, she gasped then turned on her heel and marched back inside.

"Wait... Wait... Dammit." The unexpected abruptness startled him. His hand grabbed her waist and practically lifted her back. She tried to kick and punch but her blows were ridiculously powerless. He could barely decipher her broken words and mumbles. When the elevator door opened, he practically threw her inside.

"Let go!" Two small hands pushed at his hard chest. "Let go, you big hippo."

He finally let her break free and looked at her with an odd curiosity. "Did you just call me a hippo?"

"Yes."

He frowned. "That's not nice."

"What's not nice, is you throwing me around like I'm a bunny!"

"Why the animal analogies?"

"Dev!"

It made him smile, the way she pouted like a child.

"I'm suppose to wait for Tim and Ev..." Her tongue felt loose and a bit out of control. "Evelyn"

"They left an hour ago." A pleasant beep interrupted them and the elevator doors slid open.

"What? Without me!" she screamed into his ear making him wince.

"Calm down." he tried, pressing one hand to calm the ringing in his ear. He was taking them out the exit. "I asked them to leave and told them that I'd drop you home." There was no way he was letting her go with anyone else while she was this tipsy. She was allowed to lose control only with him. No one else.

"But you're drunk too! I saw." she narrowed her eyes when he briefly massaged his forehead.

"I've had a few drinks. I am not drunk." he retorted.

"I'm not going to let you drive."

"Let me? Let me?" He laughed, deliriously, "The only thing you can let me do right now, is keep you standing up. Besides," He drew his phone out and checked the screen. "I'm not driving. I just called an Uber."

For a second her eyes grew wide then she sighed with odd resignation. "Oh, alright." she whispered, not sounding alright at all. "Do you remember my address then?"

A light quiver ran through her shoulders. He frowned and moved to slide his jacket off one arm then the next. She whined at the loss of his warm side embrace. A sound emanated from her chest, almost like a moan. Her hands unconsciously reached for him. In the next moment, a thick, heavy cloth was draped across her shoulder. She sighed with relief when his arm returned to bring her close.

"It's ridiculous that you think I'm going to let you go alone anywhere like this." He adjusted the jacket to cover as much of her body as possible. "We're going to my apartment."

Maybe it was just his imagination but she seemed to lighten considerably with relief.

Chapter 18

"You know what?" Rose spoke slowly as though voicing a slow, emerging thought, "let's take the SkyTrain!" She had yelled the last part and for the third time that night he winced, covering his ears.

Before he could recover, respond, question and dismiss, she had already snatched his phone, cancelled the Uber and shoved the phone back at him.

For a whole minute he stood blinking in disbelief. Then he blasted. "Have you gone mad? SkyTrain at this hour?"

"Oh come on. It'll be fun."

"That's exactly what people say after drinking too much."

Rose rolled her eyes. "Don't be so uptight. Come on. I'll show you how it's done."

"I've taken the train. Many times."

"Oh really?" Rose mocked, "Did you tow your BMW behind it?" She broke into a fit of giggles and started walking away.

"That doesn't make any sense at all." He scowled, slapping one hand to his forehead. "Come back here."

"No!" she chirped in a sing-song manner. "Think of how much money we'll save. My office covers my SkyTrain pass so we only have to buy your ticket. And what's more, I'll buy it for you. My treat."

"Thank you, Ms. Barnes. That's most benevolent of you."

"Isn't it, Mr. Malhotra? I think so too."

"And what about the cancelation fee that I just got charged on Uber?"

"It's better than paying whatever surcharge is going on at the moment." she sang along, happily traversing forward.

"I see. One problem though..."

She turned on her heel to look at him still rooted to his spot several feet away. "What?"

"You're going the wrong way, my dearest, ever so frugal, Ms. Barnes." he said, delicately, as if explaining something to a little child. He pointed to the street in the opposite direction. "The SkyTrain Station is that way."

A flush of embarrassment rose up her cheeks. Pursuing her lips, she quickened her steps and strode past him. He shook his head, falling in step.

The night drew darker and colder. She clutched his jacket close It smelled of him - cedar wood and forest with a hint of whiskey and something so wondrous that it reminded her of an oak tree on a rainy day...their oak tree.

"Can you even walk in those shoes? Your toes were twitching half the night." he asked.

"I'm fine." she mumbled, fighting a blush. They were walking up the stairs leading to the station. She had one hand looped around his bicep, holding on to him. For some reason she took it upon herself to educate him over the history of the SkyTrain.

"Do you know why the Expo Line is called...the Expo Line?"

"I'm sure you're going to tell me." he said, dryly.

She was unfazed. "In the beginning it was just called the SkyTrain, because the was the only train. But when the second line opened, which is the Millennium Line of course —"

"Of course."

"—the first line was given the name Expo Line. You see, historical it had been built during the World's Exposition Fair of 1986." She concluded perfectly, without slurring any of the words and raising one index finger in the manner of a history teacher.

"Thank you, Wikipedia."

She pouted and noticed only then that Dev was pulling out his ticket from the slot of the ticket kiosk. "Hey! It was going to be my treat."

He guided her towards the center of the platform. "I don't want another lesson on the history of the ticketing system or which font was used on the very first ticket."

She grinned, looking up at his annoyed face. "What is with you and public transportation? You never liked taking the bus back then either. You just wanted to bike or drive everywhere"

His face turned. Ever since he was a boy, he had learnt the very meaning of beauty from her face. One look at her and his heart weakened. The devil inside his head resurfaced, 'Kiss her.' it said. 'She wants it too. One kiss. Then you can stop.'

Temptation gave in...just a little bit. He touched her cheek with his thumb, slowly swiping against the smoothness of her skin.

The smile on her face slowly vanished, to be replaced by a vulnerable emotion. "But you always came with me in the bus, whenever I asked." Her eyes stayed on him, soft, unblinking and filled with emotion. "You never said no to me." She exhaled, her bottom lip quivering momentarily. A heaviness expanded inside her chest. "Why, Dev? Why did you never say no to me?" Without realizing what she was doing, her hands slipped through his waist, fingers curling around the fabric of his shirt. She pressed her body against his side, positioning her head in the crook of his neck.

He swallowed hard, the ache in his head growing worse. The tracks ahead were empty. There were still a few minutes left for the train to arrive. His heart was beating harder and harder and he was sure she could feel it. But she couldn't. Her mind was occupied by the muscles of his broad chest and the strong arms that held her so naturally.

"When you entered the party," she murmured, the words drumming against his pulse, "so many people flocked around you. I didn't think you'd see me at all."

A train pulled into the station, it's engine expelling a loud sound. Then it came to a slow halt.

He dipped his head lower. Tiny hairs of his stubble prickled tantalizingly against her soft cheek. She felt his words reverberating from his chest first, before his lips actually whispered them into her ear, soft and deliberate,

"Sweetheart, you were the first one I saw."

The endearment, now devoid of humor, made her tremble against him. And this time, even he knew it wasn't because of the wind.

Chapter 19

Stepping into the entry of his condo, Dev plopped her on the bench. He dropped to his knees, reached for one of her ankles and rested it on his bent thigh. He made a quick work of sliding it out of the elegant heel and proceeded with the other foot. Tossing his own shoes aside, and advanced into the kitchen. As the blood rushed in and the painful tension began to alleviate from her toes, Rose groaned with relief and followed him inside.

"What are you doing?" she asked, flabbergasted, when he reached for the bottle of whiskey and a glass.

"Best cure for headache, drink more." He replied, flippantly, pouring a shot of whiskey. He drained it in one gulp and refilled it, before setting the bottle aside. Carelessly holding his drink, he sauntered into to the living room.

The entire time in the SkyTrain, Rose had attached herself to him, clinging and tugging, making tiny sighs. Every once in a while she would look up from his shoulder and blink.

"Sleepy?" He had asked, pushing locks of hair away from her face, tucking it behind her ear.

"Not one bit." She smiled, dropping her head on his shoulder again.

There was only so much a man could take. His patience was wearing thin. He needed more alcohol to numb the devil that had gone berserk, inciting him.

'If you kiss her now, you can taste the wine she's been drinking all night.'

She was trailing behind him, shrugging his jacket off her shoulders.

"In that case, I want one too." She said, tossing the garment on one armchair.

"You've had enough." He took a seat on the couch and set the drink aside.

"I'm the one who gets to decide that."

"Sure. But still no." He shook his head at her challenging gaze, reinstating his decision.

She pursed her lip but didn't press further. Her eyes narrowed at him, making some mysterious assessment. He was too tired to pay attention so he simply sat back, closed his eyes, let his body relax.

He should've known better. Her tiny acts of rebellion always began with silence.

He did not hear her approach. He did anticipate being attacked - being smothered really - by this beautiful girl, who had all but leapt across his lap in sneaky effort to grab his glass and drain the whiskey in a quick, easy gulp.

"Oh for fuck sake!" he groaned.

She laughed, the voice bright and uncaring. It was driving him crazy. He grabbed her, and twisted her body over his lap. Her knees sunk into the couch on either side of him, the green dress riding up over her knees. He gripped her waist firmly with unyielding insistence, and jerked her close; her entire front pressed flush against his chest.

It happened so fast, she had no time to process it. One second she had been grinning and in another second her mouth was inches away from his. She lost her breath, her voice and any remaining sense of understanding. Her hands clung to him, helplessly, struggling for support. The broad length of his shoulders felt so solid, it made her quiver inside.

A wisp of air couldn't flow between them.

"I said no." he whispered angrily.

Her eyebrows furrowed. The mirth in those electric blue eyes faded.

"But I wanted to." she breathed, her lips drawn into a soft pout.

Her open admission tugged painfully at his heartstrings. Had she told him then, in that innocent voice of hers, that she wanted to zip-line from the fifty-fifth floor balcony to the liquor store across the street, he knew he would already be on his way to fetch the fucking rope. It made him angrier - this strange power she had over him.

Rose's focus wavered. Her eyes roamed over the column of his neck and strong line of his jaw. With feather light touches she drew an invisible line over his Adam's apple, watching with fascination, as it bobbled under her touch. Her path led her to the base of his throat and onto the open triangle of skin between the collar of his shirt; it had fascinated her all evening.

His hand clamped on her wrist, halting her torturous path.

"What are you doing?" The hoarseness of his voice startled her, breaking the trance. Her eyes shot up to meet his gaze and she was shocked to see that he was glaring. But beneath the anger there was something else, something weak and vulnerable

"I..." she willed to speak but was distracted again by his mouth. An exciting fear overtook her. When she wiggled her hand out of his grip, which he easily gave in, her fingers continued tracing a fresh path upward.

His jaw tightened at his complete lack of resolve to stop her.

Her demure exploration was merciless. The small, soft hand continued, trailing along his cheek towards his mouth, tickling the curve of his lips. Then she halted, letting this moment freeze, giving them the time and opportunity to pick a side.

One would think, having been intimate before, it wouldn't be this surprising. But what they had between them in that moment was a startling shock to their senses.

He knew what she wanted. He knew what he wanted. He also knew she wouldn't move and that he needed to be the first one to act. Except, a phenomenal fear loomed in his mind. For the first time in his adult life he felt a nonsensical lack of control. His mind fought against itself. The will to recognize reason was weakening fast against the temptation to give in to desperate desire.

In the end, it was the tip of her tongue that had peaked out to wet the side her lip, that gave him the last push to shut his logical side. When he spoke, the words were strained, gruff and dangerous.

"Tell me to stop." It was a both a command and a warning.

She sighed instead. Her hand dropped from his face and landed on his shoulder. Blinking softly, she drew herself closer. It was a gentle motion but it was more than enough for his control to snap.

His lips crashed on hers.

Time stopped dead. It felt like an explosion. As if a burst of high energy had shattered their whole surrounding. Or maybe it was as if a powerful force had sucked in every shred of the outside world into nothingness. The two opposites manifested at once, nullifying the endothermic and exothermic effects, until time decided to unfreeze itself.

He kissed her hard, almost brutally. His mouth consumed her with a violence that made her tremble. She was the first to make a sound - a deep, agonizing moan. It sped through his body like a raging fire. He groaned, low and dangerous, kissing her deeper still.

They broke apart for a moment. The decadent sound of erratic breathing rang through the room. He flipped them over, eliciting a loud gasp when her back collapsed into the couch. Without missing a beat, the planes of his body stretched over her delicate frame. His mouth on hers again.

He wasn't kissing. He was devouring.

A strange anguish overtook her. She was drowning and he was the only one she could hold on to. Her hands wound around his waist, clutching at his back. When his muscles twitched under her palms, she moaned with pleasure, reveling in the triumph that he burned as madly as she did. The powerful weight of his body crushed her underneath. Her body was awake and alive with sensation. The fabric of his clothing, the white button down shirt and black dress pants, rubbed against the exposed skin of her arms and thighs. She succumbed to him, giving into whatever his mouth demanded of her.

She knew then, this must be what they called, exaltation.

His hands were everywhere, blatantly entitled. He touched her like it was his right; like it was his authority and his alone, to press his hand against the curve of her waist and trail it down her thigh. The hem of her green dress had ridden up several indecent inches. His fingers hooked under one knee and hitched it higher, sinking deeper into her body. He pulled his mouth away, only momentarily, before trailing open mouthed kisses along the line of her jaw and finally descending into the curve of her neck, sucking at a delectable patch of skin.

A strangled sob emanated from her throat. Had it been a more coherent environment, she would've been mortified by it. Instead her fingers raked through his hair. Her heart pounded erratically, losing rhythm and sense. She stretched her neck, offering more of herself to him.

Somewhere in his ridiculously compromised mind, a thought persisted that they shouldn't be doing this. After all these years it would only be disastrous to continue in a drunken state. But God help him if he could find an ounce of will. The alcohol was no match for the kind of high she gave him. He was inebriate - utterly drunk on her. She tasted sweet, innocent and decadent. The shape of her body, the devilish sounds from her lips, everything about her stormed his desire. Her delicate body writhed beneath his in absolute surrender. She gave herself over to him freely, with unquestionable trust. A fierce possessiveness raked through him.

Every fire and every storm that threatened to touch her would have to deal with him first.

He knew she was far beyond the point of any coherent thought. She would've let him...wouldn't have stopped him. If anything, the way her leg was wrapped around him, she was only leading them further down the path.

He tore his mouth away from her skin, every intention of stopping. But she whimpered loudly; disappointment etched on her face and red swollen lips curved petulantly. She reached for him, fingers curling around his shirt. She looked irresistible and adorable, a combination that wrenched at his heart, making it impossible to deny her in any manner.

Whatever power he had over his world, all that came crashing down in front of her. It always did.

His body lowered overs hers again. pressing his lips on the side of her neck. She sighed audibly, pacified by his touch. His rough palm stroked her leg, setting her skin on fire in it's wake. His mouth became hotter and bolder, kissing and sucking, eliciting indecent whimpers from her. She didn't know how or when but at some point she realized that her dress was hitched dangerously higher and his hand was stroking the side of her thigh. It terrified her further to realize that she was halfway through unbuttoning his shirt.

She let her hands roam freely over his chest, hard muscles twitching beneath her soft palms. His shirt lay open and she was tugging at the collar, trying to slid it over his shoulders. Then in a moment of sheer insanity, she did something that would haunt and excite her for many days to come.

She reached into the crook of his neck and sunk her teeth, biting him.

He swore under his breath. For a moment the shock stilled him. A deeply, masculine sound vibrated from his chest. Then his hand dug into her thigh.

"Fuck...sweetheart" he growled against her skin. His mouth grew hotter and bolder, traveling down her neck. Lower and lower.

"Dev."

His name came out as a breathless moan carrying with it too many emotions - a plea, a request, an apology...

"Dev..."

...an echo of a time that was past but never forgotten. And a present that was threatening to plunge them into an abyss of uncertainty.

The sound of his name travelled to the depths of his soul. It now held a feeling that was too deep, too dangerous, too meaningful and so entirely evident that it could no longer be ignored.

And that is what made him stop.

He halted, freezing the air around them. Every instinct in his body was mad with desire. It took inhuman resolve to let go of her, to loosen his grip and pull away. The room was filled with the sounds of their ragged breathing. The moments stretched painfully. His head hovered overs hers, peering into the electric blue of her eyes. He pressed his lips to her forehead in a long, lingering kiss. When his breath began to even, he turned them over; his back to the couch, his arms cradling her body.

She wanted to cry. Sadness, embarrassment and fear rampaged through her mind. His shirt was still unbuttoned. She buried herself into his chest, curling her arms and legs, trying to make her body as small as possible. She remained lifeless and passive when the hem of her dress was smoothened and when his hand stroked her hair. He was holding her protectively now, like she was infinitely fragile and an inch away from shattering into piece s...which wasn't all together false. For days to come, this night would be a source of much confusion and anxiety but for now, she sought comfort in his arms.

Sometime later, he disentangled their bodies and rose. She remained curled on the couch, eyes shut tight, almost asleep. But he knew she wasn't. He bent lower and slipped one hand underneath her knees, the other under her back. Like a limp doll, she let him move her and simply dropped her head on his shoulder, when he carried her inside. It was only when she was gently placed onto a soft mattress and he seemed to pull away, did her eyes spring open with surprising urgency.

"Don't go." she murmured, her voice meek with fear.

It broke his heart. He leaned over her, holding the side of her cheek in his hand.

"I'm not going to leave you." Ever. "I'm just going to change and bring you some clothes."

She realized then, that she was on his bed, in his room.

A minute later he appeared from the guest bedroom with her pajamas, which must've gotten left behind on some past evening. Handing it to her, he turned to the bathroom.

By the time he returned, dressed in track pants and a t-shirt, she had changed out of her dress and was lying on the bed, curled to one side. He got in and promptly reached for her.

"Come here." he whispered, stretching one arm. She complied instantly and he pulled the covers over.

They fell asleep, holding each other.

Chapter 20

Rose awoke in the morning to an eerie silence and an empty bed. The curtains were drawn but the sun still fought its way through, flittering tiny spokes of light onto the bed. Next to her the sheets were rumpled and the pillow still smelled of Dev. There was a strange comfort in waking up in his bed but also a distinct coldness that he wasn't in it.

She made her way into the living room. Even her light footfalls felt more pronounced in the dim quietness. She wouldn't be surprised if Dev had actually stepped out of his apartment.

But he was there. Reclined on the couch and breathing gently. She walked gingerly, afraid to break the peace with one small misstep. He was staring out the massive window and continued to do so when she came to stand in front of him. For long moments, they simply remained, inactive and unthinking.

Finally, his words emerged from the tranquil silence. "Do you want to know how I feel?"

Once before, he had asked her that question. She had refused him then. She had turned her back to the truth. Today she remained silent.

He wasn't going to make this easier for her. "Do you want to tell me how you feel?"

"Yes." Her voice seemed to echo, as if someone else had uttered the word from a far distance.

"Sit." he whispered, still looking outside.

Her knees buckled and she lowered onto the armchair behind.

He didn't prod her. He waited, calm and unhurried.

"Dev...I..." she began but her throat pained with heaviness. "I don't how..." A shaky exhale escaped her. "How do I say it?"

He finally turned to look at her. His face was unreadable; he gave nothing away.

"I've never judged you, Ro and I won't start now. You can say whatever you want, however you want to." His body remained still, only his eyelids blinked. "It's just me."

She chuckled in a sad, humorless way. "Ironic isn't it? That I'm asking you to help me even here? It seems like I'm always the one asking for help."

"Do we need to keep an account on who seeks help and how often? And incidentally, if we were to keep a score then I've far outnumbered you."

"That's not true. I'm always the one taking from you, never able to give you anything."

"Rose." His voice was hard. "Our entire young lives, I have only taken from you. Purpose, inspiration, ambition...everything I took from you."

"No!" she cried, suddenly inflamed. "You haven't. As far back as I can remember, you looked after me. Everything I did, everywhere I went, you were right there behind me, beside me, in front of me, caring for me even when..." Her chest constricted painfully. "even when I asked you not to."

"So what?" he clenched his teeth. His eyes snapped to hers. "So what if I did?"

"How do I make you understand?" Her eyes darted around the room, searching for some source of reason, some piece of logic that could help her. She needed to say it, needed to explain it to me and maybe then it would be less painful.

She took a breath and let the flood of her thoughts flow by:

"Every time I think about high school I just want to cry. There's so much I'd set out to do. Everyone around me had thought the I'd achieve something big, something brilliant. Even you," Her stare pierced into his, "You used to admire me. You looked up to. Once. What did I do with it? With all that hope and expectation? I bombed it! I squashed every thread of potential around me. All for the sake of doing something big and extraordinary. The only thing I succeeded at was to make a muck out of the ordinary things. In my pursuit of these big dreams, in chasing something phenomenal, I didn't value what was in front of me. Whatever state I am in now, I deserve it! My ego, my pride is the reason I hurt you! And now," her eyes fell, staring at her lap, "Look at me now, Dev. There's nothing left to admire. You'll never be able to see me like you used to. And it hurts to think of it because," Her hands had gotten too heavy and she let them fall to her sides, "because I admire you. So very much. You're wonderful and so..." she bit her bottom lip. "I don't have the right words for it. Its just...I cannot go through life knowing you don't think of me that way and possibly never would."

She didn't want to continue. This was too painful to admit. But it needed to be said out loud.

"I feel so small. The things you've achieved, the person that you've become - I'm nothing in front of it. You could be with anyone, just about anyone. And I can't help but think, why would you want to settle with me." The words chocked in her throat "The truth is, your world is much bigger and better than mine. And there is no place for me in it."

A silence followed like a numbing calmness that emerges in the wake of turbulent storm. She wasn't looking at him or else she would've seen that he was visibly aghast. His chest wrung painfully. He felt helpless. Her words carried conviction and surety. She actually believed what she said. And that shocked him. He wanted to take her out of her misery. He just didn't know how.

It took him a while to gather his thoughts and form a coherent response.

"In the last eight years if your life had gone differently, if you had done well at school and got the perfect job, would you have regretted your decisions?" He had asked the question with calculated calmness but a surge of anger was boiling inside him. "Answer me." he demanded.

Her hands clasped together in her lap, eyes downcast.

"You won't answer, I know. So I'll do it for you. You carry regret because you feel your decisions alone led you to failure. They didn't. You haven't understood that sometimes, bad circumstances defeat even the strongest of people, despite their best efforts. Your circumstances don't define you. They're fleeting like the wind. When clouds overcast a sky, you don't doubt, even for a second, that the sky isn't beautiful. You simply wait for the clouds to clear. The sky is forever blue and always beautiful."

He wasn't expecting her to respond at all, anymore.

"You feel that your failures are your punishment for your mistakes. You hurt me, so now you must suffer - that's what your mind is telling you. Yes, I was hurt. But you were hurting inside too. I knew that and yet I still let go of you. We pushed and pulled and in the end gave up. That was the mistake - our mistake that we made together."

He was sitting up now, leaning forward, piercing into her soul with his solid brown eyes. Even the air seemed to have settled around them as if it needed to pause and listen to words that came out of this man. "Tell me something. Had our story been reversed, had I been the one in need of help and you, in a position to do so, would you have judged me?"

Every muscle, every cell in her body had became numb.

He wasn't finished. "Let me push it further. If ten years from now, I lose everything, my fortune, my wealth and all this so called success that has you feeling miserable - if I lose all of this, will you think less of me? Will you not care for me? Will you not lo..." The words broke in his throat. He looked away. "This belief - that is your mistake. You're wrong, Rose."

When she blinked, something hot and heavy squeezed out of her eyes. Then her cheeks felt wet. It was too tiring and difficult to maintain a sitting posture. Someone needed to open the windows. She was finding it hard to breath.

With the sleeve of one forearm, she wiped her tears. Her body straightened and moved toward the hallway. He slumped back into the couch and covered his eyes with one palm. When she emerged shortly after, changed and holding a handbag, he did not move. Their eyes met one last time. Her breath wavered, choking back a silent sob. Then she turned around and left.

Chapter 21

The days that followed were difficult and forlorn. Rose buried herself in work, taking more tasks than any assistant ever had. Her colleagues watched her with concern and Simon Banfield grew weary. He briefly considered taking to Cary and having Rose be taken off some tasks. But the girl's determination was too sincere and he decided to give her some time.

Dev's twelve-hour work days grew to fourteen, even fifteen. His conversations with people were limited and specific. At one point his mom worried that he may be ill. His little sister Annie tried to question if this had something to do with Rose. She had met Rose once while visiting his apartment and had been anxious ever sense. He ignored her prying questions.

It was an unlikely person who knocked on Dev's door on a Saturday morning.

"Nia?" Dev exclaimed. He was in his pajamas. His face worn out, circles under his eyes indicating minimal hours of sleep. Before he could gather enough energy to greet or wonder, Nia had ushered herself inside.

"I thought I needed to catch up with my cousin." she said, far too brightly for his half-sleepy disposition. She looked surprising fresh, in her light denims and red sweater.

He followed, yawning.

"Here" Nia kept a mid-sized brown box, that said Victoria Bakery, on his coffee table. Dev returned to his spot on the couch and watched the open box of baked goodies, all his favorites - banana bread slice with pecans, almond croissants with chocolate, a strawberry scone and a couple of cake pops. He grew instantly suspicious. He looked from the open box to Nia, who was sitting next to him, casually sipping a cup of coffee.

Nia was pretty, in her own way. Her clothes were never overtly revealing or ostentatious. They were subtle, expensive and fine quality with a subdued theme as if the wearer aimed to hide her self. It worked for her, for the most part. At first glance, no one noticed anything remotely impressive about her. But once they saw her, really saw, once they heard her thoughts, and knew the kind of person she was, it was impossible to look away. She casually hid her charming personality under a highly wound box of politeness and reservations.

Amongst all his cousins, Dev felt most comfortable with her. She had a knack for getting people to confide in her without obvious probing. Her quiet, open nature made her trust worthy and safe. She was only a year younger than Dev. Somehow, through the years they'd shared parts of their lives with each other. Even though she had an older brother and Dev had Annie, Nia and Dev had a genuine bond of familial affection. They understood each other.

Dev's gaze dropped to the open box again, then rose back up to Nia.

Down to the box. Then up to his cousin.

Down. up.

Down. up.

"No matter how many times you look it'll still be there." Nia chirped, smiling sweetly.

"This is for me?" he asked, pointing to the box.

"Yeah."

"You brought this for me?"

"Yeah."

"To eat?"

Nia huffed, rolling her eyes. "Why are you being so dramatic?"

"Because the oatmeal girl is offering me this," he picked up on one scone with two fingers, like it was a specimen to be examined, "this tiny mountain of sugar." He set it back in the box. "So excuse me for being a tiny bit shocked."

"Oh God," she waved one hand, rolling her eyes and took a sip of her coffee. "You know how early I had to get up to make it to Victoria's? They sell out of their croissants so fast. I actually wanted to try the brownies but..."

"Brownies?" Dev's eyes grew wide. He pressed one hand to his face, shaking his head with a defeated sigh. "Drop this."

"Drop what?"

He glanced at her. "You wouldn't be caught dead with a cookie, let alone a full brownie. Your idea of a cheat-day is to put honey in your god-awful smoothies."

"That's ridiculous. I always put a little honey in my smoothies."

A hint of annoyance entered his voice. "What," he emphasized, "is going on?!"

Nia had thought bringing him his favorite treats for breakfast would help to start the difficult conversation. Clearly she'd been mistaken. Sighing, she set the coffee on the table and straightened herself. "I'm worried about you."

Dev groaned. In the past three weeks, he'd heard that statement more times than he'd care to listen. "Not you too." He tried to turn his attention back to the screen, but Nia reached to shut his laptop.

"Dev, you have to talk to me first."

"Talk about what?!" he asked, irritated. Grabbing a handful of a plush throw blanket, he carelessly draped it over himself. As an after thought, he pulled the material over his head, covering his face.

"Very mature." Nia rolled her eyes.

"Leave me alone." came a tired, muffled voice from underneath the blanket. With a quick motion, she pulled the blanket away from his face.

He pulled it back up.

"Stop being childish." Nia tugged firmly, pulling it completely off. His head was tipped back and body loose, tired with an unnamed exhaustion.

She tugged at his shirt with affection. "Whatever it is, you can tell me."

He rolled his head sideways. "Nothing and maybe everything." he whispered, quietly. "I feel like a building is slowly crumbling, one wooden beam at a time, and I am standing somewhere far, unable to stop that disaster."

"Rose?" Nia asked, as if that one name was enough to hold an entire question.

Dev nodded.

"Um..." Nia hesitated for a moment, before asking, "Are you sure what you're feeling is real?"

Dev looked at her, puzzled.

"You could just be falling into an old comfort zone with someone you once loved and clearly never stopped caring." Fearing he may get angry, she continued quickly, explaining, "You and Rose have this history. You once believed you were meant to be together. So now, all these years later, maybe your mind is trying to recapture that teenage dream in a world that's not the same. It's possible she's doing the same thing. What concerns me, is that if you guys get together, then realize that reality isn't matching up to your dreams, the damage that will follow could be irreparable."

She paused, placing one hand on his forearm and giving him a warm squeeze. "If you two were to end things again...I fear, you would break inside. You both might suffer more than you can heal or mend."

He felt the plush throw blanket being draped over him again. Next the open brown box was placed on his lap. He sat up a little and wordlessly picked up a scone. He took a small bite. A shot of sweetness entered his body. He realized only then that he had been quite hungry. He focused on eating the scone one bite after bite. Nia reached for the second cup of coffee and offered it to him.

"Really?" Dev asked, taking a sip, a ghost of smile on his face.

"Even I have my limits." she grinned, in response to non-fat sugarless latte that she hadn't been able to resist ordering for him.

Dev picked up the croissant next tore it in half. He gave Nia the half without the chocolate coating. They ate in silence, sipping on their coffees.

The box was emptied soon. A renewed energy emerged inside him with a sugary dose of food and coffee.

Nia spoke again. "I asked you this not to complicate things further. I really," she said with earnestness, "really want to help you. And if having an unpleasant conversation is going to help, then let's do. I just want you to think about this carefully."

Dev gave her a slow, affectionate smile. "Thanks Nia."

"You don't have to thank me. You know what we always say. Blood makes us family but we chose to be brother and sister...I don't want to see you falling into an abyss." she paused. "or Rose for that matter. She's a good human being and I truly believe she cares for you. But is it at all possible, that this is it...There's nothing else beyond this. Maybe this is where your story is supposed to end?"

When he answered, his voice was heavy. "It's possible."

"Then?"

For the past three weeks, a constant though process had been running in Dev's mind. He dropped his head back on the couch, feet perched on the coffee table ahead. His hands were limp, resting on the sides. Nia turned to lean back next to him, following his line of sight at the ceiling above.

He spoke, staring at the ceiling. "I don't care."

Every thought, every doubt and every possibility always yielded only one conclusion

"I don't care if it seems like she's my comfort zone. I don't care that we failed before. In some way, we had vowed never to see each other again. And yet here we are. Now that I've known her, all over again, I've realized that there is no way...no fucking way that our story had ended. What happened back then...it was only a chapter...an interlude. A sad one, I admit. But not the end. The interlude just lasted a lot longer."

His voice changed. It carried a quiet resolve that was unshakable, almost like a solemn oath. "I'm ending this interlude. I don't care where our story is supposed to go. Because I'm not waiting to read it anymore. I'm going to write it. The last time we stopped trying. This time I'm not going down without a fight. Our destiny is just a series of choices that we are too afraid to make. I'm not afraid...not anymore."

****

Rose waited anxiously inside a charming little Italian bistro. She had been astonished to receive this brunch invitation from an unlikely person. Interactions with Nia had been usually limited around a single commonality; the said 'commonality' with whom Rose hadn't spoken to in three weeks.

Nia waved to her from the entrance and approached the table. "Thanks for coming. I know this must be surprising."

"Yeah, but I'm happy you did." Rose replied. "I don't get out much."

The server took their orders and the food arrived fairly quickly. Nia had picked the place. The food was delicious but a bit on the expensive side. She had expected it, though since Dev had already told her about his cousin (warned her, really.) They spoke casually about the recent surge in house prices, all the while Rose anticipating the conversation which was the real reason for this brunch.

"There's something I want to talk to you about."

Rose set her fork down. "It's about Dev, isn't it?"

"Yes. But it's also about you." Nia paused. "How are you?"

Rose sighed. "I'm alright. How is he?"

"The same."

A short silence followed, the surrounding chatter filling the silence on the table.

"Do you know about the Annual Racing Cup at Hastings?" Nia said in between of morsels.

Rose shook her head.

"It's a horse racing event. Takes place once a year. Our family and a few others have large VIP boxes pre booked. You should come."

Rose's eyes grew wide with open surprise. "What do you mean?"

"Come for the event. The races are an excuse, it's more of a social gathering with fancy hats and a lot of booze." Nia grinned. "And after that, we go Roman's beach house for the evening."

Rose pursued her lip, taken aback. "Nia..." she hesitated, "how can I just show up? Uninvited..."

"I am inviting you. Believe me, there's so much action and noise, people will hardly realize you're there in the first place."

"I don't know." Rose shook her head, apprehensively. "It doesn't make any sense for me to go. I'll be so out of place. Besides these things are expensive. I don't think I can afford to pay for the ticket, let alone the food and drinks."

Nia responded eagerly. "You'll be my guest Rose. You don't have to pay for anything. Our family invitations are extended to so many friends and peers, you won't be out of place at all."

Rose bit her bottom lip, considering the idea. "I can try for the event but...um...not the after party. I can't simply walk into someone's house."

"It's not someone else. It's just Roman. You must've heard Dev mention him."

"Yeah." Rose had virtually met him to be precise, but she didn't feel like explaining all that.

"See, not a stranger then." Nia pointed. "He has a huge house in Kitsilano. Every now and then he throws a party. Believe me, at this point even Roman has lost track of who gets invited when."

Rose remained silent, looking confused.

"Nia," she began, "I'm grateful to you for inviting me. It's very thoughtful. But really," she bit her lip, "there isn't a good reason for me to go."

"I have a very good reason actually." said Nia said, holding her gaze, "You can't ignore Dev forever. Whatever this is, between you and Dev, it needs to be said out loud for both of you to deal with it. Uncertainty helps no one."

The delicious pasta in front of Rose has lost its appeal. "I have no idea what to say to him."

"You'll find the words, or maybe you'll find a way to coexist without carrying the weight of the world on your shoulders. Whatever it is, give it a try sooner than later."

The idea was preposterous, ridiculous in every way, save for one - she wanted to see him.

"I bet Dev will be shocked if I show up." she said with a sad smile.

"Maybe not."

"I think so. And he might not want to talk to me yet."

"I can say with some confidence, that he won't be surprised to see you. And that he'll definitely talk to you."

"Why?"

"Because he's one who suggested it." Nia replied with a sense of finality, ending all further discussion.

Chapter 22

The Hastings Cup was Vancouver's answer to the Kentucky Derby. To begin with, it was crowded. A sea of hats, fascinators and berets swam through the stands. And the clothes! Rose had rarely seen people stick to the theme with such precision - fashionable day dresses, high heels and dapper suits. The area was energized with the upbeat music from a live band while the air smelled of mud, horses, alcohol and the warm summer sun.

Nia guided her through the stands towards a section on the west side. "This is our private booth!" She said. They stepped into a decent-sized room with a glass wall, overlooking the tracks. Tables and chairs were laid out, a bar was situated at the corner, and people walked about socializing. It was calmer here, more orderly.

"If you're looking for a more raw experience, there's another spot as well." Nia explained. They stepped out of the booth and a good twenty steps below. Right in front of the main tracks stood a large canopy. It was the best and closest spot to view the race. Six tables and numerous chairs lay underneath it, though hardly any of the chairs were occupied as people huddled at the railing.

A well-dressed young man appeared and before Nia could introduce them, he had hurried her away, leaving Rose alone. She didn't mind it though. This was quiet a lot to take in and she was glad to find a moment to herself. Before she realized what she was doing, her gaze travelled across the crowd looking for one face. She didn't have to wait for long.

"Boo!" Dev exclaimed very close to her ear. It was so silly - A boo! - really? Like they were five years old. But somehow it melted her apprehension and she broke into a smile. She turned to find herself looking up at a familiar handsome face which had featured in her dreams far too many times in the past three weeks.

"I'm glad you came." He said, tilting his head.

"Thank you for inviting me." How she had missed him!

"Nia invited you."

Pursuing her lips, Rose gave him a meaningful glance.

He winked. "Your welcome. Let's get something to drink."

Dev looked ridiculously attractive in a light sky blue suit, white shirt and brown shoes. He didn't wear a hat like some of the men but instead chose dark sunglasses. With drinks in their hands they returned to stand by the railing, watching the race tracks.

"I'm sorry I haven't really spoken to you properly for a while." Rose began. "I wasn't sure..."

"No, don't apologize." he said.

The sound of hooves echoed. From a distance, five small ponies appeared being guided by their masters. The crowd cheered and applauded as the young mares took a lap around the track.

"What's happening?" She asked.

"Foals." Dev replied, bringing the glass to his lips. "Someday they'll race too."

Rose shook her head in disapproval.

Dev cast her knowing glance, half a smile curved along the side of his face. "They're treated well. We make sure of it."

"We?" Rose's lifted one eyebrow. "You own these horses?" It was more of an accusation than question.

"Not exactly. My family makes yearly contributions. The funds are used to care for the horses and maintain the stables."

"So...you own them?"

Dev chuckled, taking a sip from his glass.

Rose shook her head. Contributing to horses! It was such a rich thing to do.

His gaze stayed on the shape of her lips when she pouted with annoyance. "You know my dad was completely against the idea at first. It took me a while to convince him. In the end I think he only agreed because it was a good opportunity to network and strengthen his social status."

"Since when have you cared about horses, anyway? You weren't interest before." The beautiful foals were now passing right below them. They looked healthy and well groomed, Rose noticed. "I remember." Her eyebrows scrunched at a long forgotten memory. "There was this stable across town that belonged to Mr. Nelson...he was such a character. I hated him. Never kept the place clean. He was so cruel to his horses. I used to badger you all the time, even when we had a lot of homework left. God, I must've annoyed you so much."

"You never annoyed me."

Something fluttered in her stomach and she fought the urge to blush. "There was this small pony...what was his name?" She squinted her eyes thoughtfully.

He shook his head, taking a sip from his glass.

"Anyway, I distinctly remember trying to sneak him out to set him free." She laughed, softly. "It was such a stupid thing to do. Dad had to pay Mr. Nelson, just so the incident could be finished right then. And mom had to hear him complain for god knows how long. In fact, he wanted to shout at me but you..." Rose's breath hitched. The words were caught in her chest.

But you wouldn't let him.

An image flashed - a fifteen-year-old Dev marching across a dirty field to threaten a grouchy stable master that if anyone raised their voice at Rose, he would call more government officials than they had the money to deal with. Dev hadn't known any government officials. But Rose had been sure that he would've managed to make true on that threat.

Dev for his part, however, had completely missed her words. He was mulling over something else entirely.

A female voice blared from the speakers, announcing that the first race was about to commence. The field broke into an applause. Several others came to stand on either side of then, inadvertently pushing them closer. His shoulder was overlapping hers. The side of their bodies were glued, bartering warmth and smell; she, of sweet summer flowers and he, of cedar wood and forest.

The mares were lined up at the starting gate. The sound of a bullet shot through the sky and all at once, the fillies took off. It was a sight to behold, indeed. Seven horses ran at a frightening pace. The chants and cheers from the crowd grew louder. When the horses passed by them, a cloud of dust rose high in their wake, causing a few to cough out the dust. Dev's eyes followed number nine. It was leading in the top three. He sighed. When he'd asked Nia to invite Rose here, number nine wasn't suppose to run at all. It was changed on short notice which he now regretted approving without paying attention. His eyes closed, praying the horse didn't win.

Number nine came second.

He grimaced, dreading the announcement that was sure to follow.

".... on the second place we have Wellington, the proud mare from the Malhotra family."

Her heart stopped. A shiver ran through her body. Her limbs felt frozen and heavy. A part of her mind tried to entertain the idea that maybe she had misheard the announcement. She turned to look up at Dev but he had disappeared. She was alone, looking at the track where a horse had sped past moments ago.

A horse who was named Wellington.

The name came crashing back...the name of the pony she had tried to rescue. The name that minutes ago Dev didn't seem to recollect.

No. It couldn't be. It's just a coincidence.

Dev hadn't expected their conversation to turn that way. Four years ago Nia had introduced the idea that an organization was looking for generous sponsors to save horses from deteriorating stables and revive this old race course. Nia loved horses, he didn't. But he had agreed on impulse. A myriad of emotions lay underneath - anger, spite, longing, loyalty and even a bit of ego. His best friend had vanished from his life. All he had was her memory and his mind fought to keep it alive in any and every way possible. At that point, there had been no hope for her return. But she was here now, dressed in shades of yellow, looking like the first rays of sunrise. And at the moment, she was standing non-pulsed at the proof of his pathetic obsession.

Dev hid himself in a far corner of the VIP booth, lamenting that their first meeting after weeks of silence had commenced so awkwardly.

A hand clapped on his shoulder.

"You won!" Roman exclaimed, taking a seat next to him. A maroon checkered suit didn't sit well on most men. Roman, however, wasn't one of them. Maroon checkered, pink stripes, brown polka dots or lime herringbone, Roman could make any color and any pattern seem in vogue.

"Yeah, I suppose." Dev muttered.

"Winning usually makes people quite happy." When Roman only gave a non committal 'hmm' in responses, he continued, "I wonder, if this Grinch-like behavior has anything to do with that pretty one in yellow?"

"Not in the mood." Dev gritted through his teeth.

"Clearly." Roman contemplated. "Here's what I think."

"I don't remember asking for your opinion."

"Oh but I'm always willing to bestow my opinions to friends, absolutely free. So you might as well take it."

Dev sighed, blinking with annoyance.

"So, your high school girlfriend right there..."

"What!"

"That one," Roman explained, gesturing to Rose as if specific details were needed. "she's wearing that yellow dress with a brown hat. Quite stunning actually..."

"I know who you're talking about." Dev glared.

"Oh good. Nash and I had quite a discussion about her the other day."

"Why were both of you discussing her?"

"Well, to be fair, we were discussing you and her, as one entity."

"One entity? Wonderful" Dev laughed humorlessly.

"Do you deny it? You've been spending an awful amount of time together. She's at your place every other evening. And after the Foxridge party, people have started talking."

Dev's eyes narrowed. "Which people have started talking what?"

"Just this and that." Roman waved one hand casually.

"Roman..."

"Alright. I received some pictures from the party and I couldn't help but notice how you and your non-ex-girlfriend were a tiny bit" The pause felt patronizing, "cozy."

"I want to see these pictures."

"Not a chance. And don't think about asking Nash, he won't send them to you either."

Dev was about to yell in frustration again but held himself back. "What friends I have." he muttered, crossing both arms over his chest. "Gossiping about my love-life like a bunch of jobless old aunties."

"At least you're willing to admit it's your love life."

Dev clenched his teeth, throwing daggers at his friend.

"It wasn't a gossip session." Roman said. "Not at first at least. Arsenal lost, so naturally I wanted to rub some salt in Nash's wounds. Now that I think about it, I actually called you as well. We thought we'd do a conference. It was just last week. You didn't answer."

Dev looked at him, incredulously. "That was the conference? It was three-thirty in the morning!"

"Not for us. You were the only on on Pacific time zone then."

"Oh yeah... how stupid I am to sleep in my own bed in the middle of the night while the two of you were busy... wait... last week. Fuck, I spoke to Nash two days ago. Bastard! Didn't say a single word."

"Well, in Nash's case it'd be more surprising if he had said something."

Dev grudgingly agreed. "Well, what was the conclusion of your discussion?"

A roguish grin spread across Roman's face. "Considering both of us were half distracted by the game, it is quite obvious that we came to absolutely no conclusion."

"Then why did you bring it up in the first place!"

"I didn't bring it up..." Roman said, thoughtfully. "The conversation just went in that direction."

Dev groaned. "I should know." He ran his hand through his hair, muttering to himself. "Conversations are going in all sorts of directions today."

"What?"

"Nothing."

"Let's get back to the topic then."

"Really?"

"Yes, really." Roman stated, squinting his eyes to recollect his train of thought. "So Rose, your high school girlfriend..."

"We never officially dated so no, that's not true."

Roman chuckled. "You can convince yourself all you want and find excuses but... Oh, there they go again." Roman commented on another round of the race that had just begun.

Dev's eyes trailed the path ahead.

After the horses had passed, Roman spoke. "You can complicate this as much as you like. But in the end it will come down to only one thing."

"Why did you never tell me before, Roman?" Dev asked, slightly high pitched and cheerful.

Roman startled. "Tell you what?"

"That while you were majoring in Civil Engineering, you minored in Psychology?"

Roman rolled his eyes, retorting dryly, "At least I'm not letting my old girlfriend get under my skin."

"She was never my gi..."

"Shut up for fuck sake." Roman waved his hand in front of Dev's face, physically dismissing him. "You're ready to pounce on her and she's turning red at the sight of you. Please," He implored, shaking his head, "just listen."

Dev's jaw clenched but he remained silent, letting Roman continue.

"Whatever you guys did before, it's gone. Forever. If you want her now, in this moment, in this time, then tell her. You can brood and over think this a million times and it will get you nothing."

The race had ended. The winners were announced and people retreated for a short break before another race commenced. Dev saw Rose being whisked away by Nia. She stood awkwardly amongst Nia's friends, speaking with hesitation. Mostly, she just smiled and nodded. Every now and then, her gaze would drift away as if looking for something or someone. When she finally found Dev, she turned away quickly, a deep blush emerging on her cheeks.

Dev's heart beat painfully in his chest. He wanted to be the one to whisk her away, take her to meet his friends, make her feel safe and comfortable so she would do more than just smile. He wanted to touch her, readjust the hat that had fallen from it's careful arrangement on her head, swipe that stray lock of hair troubling her eyes...

"Wow" Roman exclaimed softly, pulling Dev from his thoughts. "You're done for, mate."

This time Dev didn't deny it. He was tired and he really, really wanted to hold her.

"Tell her, Dev." Roman whispered, no humor in his voice, just a carefully concealed affection.

"She knows."

"And?"

Dev paused, his eyes on the stunning girl in yellow. "She's afraid."

Roman didn't reply.

****

"It was exciting, wasn't it?" Nia's face glowed with excitement.

Rose nodded with a smile.

"Are you hungry?"

"No, I'm alright. What happens next?"

"There's a break now for about twenty minutes before the next race begins."

"Have you bet on any of the horses?"

"Me? Oh God, no." Nia laughed. "I'm not into betting at all. I'm just fond of horses."

"Do you come here often? Dev said your family is one of the sponsors."

"Every now and then, yes. I come here just to check on the horses, take one for a walk, spend an afternoon, that kind of thing."

Unconsciously Rose looked at Dev again, standing far inside the VIP booth. He was now talking to a woman in a fashionable white dress. She wore a dramatic red hat with a large flower made of lace and beads; the whole piece was twice the side of her head. But she made it look spectacular. She was young, polished, and entirely too beautiful.

Rose was generally quite comfortable in her skin, even when money was scarce to throw around for aesthetic self care. So another woman's beauty didn't make her feel easily insecure.

No, it wasn't the woman's appearance that caused a burning sensation in her chest. It was the fact that the woman had her hand looped around Dev's arm.

Second time, she whispered to herself.

A little while ago, she'd noticed Dev talking to a group of friends, the woman in white being one of them. She spoke enthusiastically and Dev had laughed. It didn't bother Rose then. But it did now. Because he was letting her cling to him. To make matters worse, he placed his hand over hers, patting it.

Envy surged inside her. The feeling was so sudden and intense that she was momentarily numbed by it. They were probably just friends. Hell, she could even be one of his many cousins. Though, considering the way she winked at him, that possibility was low. In any case, there was no logical reason for her to become so breathless with rage.

"Who is that?" she asked, unable to ignore her curiosity any longer.

"That..." Nia squinted her eyes for a second. "That's Aniya Grewal. She's a family friend. Why?"

"No reason." Rose muttered, in a failed attempt to sound nonchalant.

From distance, Roman's eyes coasted from Dev to Aniya to Rose.

He smirked.

Chapter 23

- -

Aniya Grewal had made herself very comfortable next to Dev. They were sitting on one of the far tables and her hand was gently stroking his left bicep. She had leaned in and was talking in low whispers, forcing Dev to get closer just so he could hear her properly. She smiled every once in a while, randomly, without cause.

"You seem oddly happy today." Dev asked, looking curiously at his old friend.

Aniya giggled dramatically, causing Dev to raise an eyebrow. Then she leaned in further and propped her chin on his shoulder in a manner that she'd never done before.

"I had a very interesting conversation with Roman just minutes ago." she whispered, then winked.

For a good long minute, Dev looked dumbfounded. Then his eyes grew wide as the implication registered in his mind. One hand slapped his forehead, then trailed along the side of his face, as if the movement would wipe away his quickly rising anger.

"For the love of God," he seethed, "I'm going to kill that..."

"Relax." Aniya chirped, tightening her hold on his bicep, practically snuggling. "Just play along."

"Play...pla..." His disbelief and rage left him grappling for words. He took a breath then bore his eyes into hers. Ironically, that solidified their intimate stance.

"What exactly did Roman tell you?" he snapped.

"Unfortunately, not as much as I would like to know." She admitted, gently caressing his bicep.

"Stop that!"

"What?" she asked with mock innocence, then renewed her movements more dramatically, "Oh, you mean, this."

Dev glared.

"Roman told me he was doing an experiment. All I had to do was go up and," Twisting her head, she rested her chin on his shoulder to smile coyly at him. "snuggle for a few minutes."

Dev remained motionless, stunned at the ridiculousness of the situation. "And you agreed to this because?"

"To make my afternoon more entertaining." Her head fell on his shoulder. "Besides, I'm curious to know more about this experiment."

Beneath the refuge of his sunglasses, he stole a glance at his Rose. She was trying and failing quite miserably, to ignore him. Every time her eyes shot to the corner, the anxiety on her face deepened.

"I'm going to tell Jack about this." Dev grumbled

Aniya didn't reply right away. For a moment, Dev thought she'd actually fallen asleep.

"Oh he knows." Aniya said, lazily. "Your shoulder is actually quite comfortable."

"More comfortable than your boyfriend's shoulder?"

"Ha... you wish."

"Where is Jack, anyway?"

She lifted her head and scoured the area, one hand shielding her eyes from the bright sunlight.

"He said he was going to take pictures." she whispered. "I can't see him though."

"Pictures!" Dev's sense of composure was slipping further away by the minute.

"Of course. If the experiment is successful, then this story is going to be passed on to our kids. I need solid proof. Ten years from now, imagine my Instagram post - Throwback to the Hastings experiment." She looked smug with her own delusions leaving Dev in a stunned silence. Then to his horror, she bent lower to kiss his cheek. It was a small, quick kiss, but enough to mortify him.

"You realize this is a very public place."

"We've been friends for so long, darling. No one's going to bat an eye. Especially since almost everyone also knows Jack is going to propose soon."

"And does Jack know that you know about that?"

"Of course not." She grinned, haughtily. "See, the thing is, I didn't get any drama or experiments in my relationship. So at the very least, before we plunge into marriage, I'm going to confuse the hell out of my husband-to-be."

"Aniya" Dev reproached, dismally. "You're a wonderful person but you've got a whole lot of crazy beneath it."

Aniya glowed at what was clearly not meant as a compliment.

Somewhere in the crowd, Roman made a cryptic gesture.

"Oh, that's my cue." she observed, almost disappointed. "Looks like I'm off stage."

"Finally." Dev muttered under his breath.

"Cheer up." she rose and straightened her dress. "And listen, I'm not going to badger you...yet. But after all this is done, tonight at Roman's beach party, I want to meet this girl who's got Dev Malhotra in a fix."

The little interest that Rose had in watching the races had all but vanished. This surge of emotion was overwhelming - envy mingled with hurt. It muddled her thoughts. She retreated into the background, finding an inconspicuous corner to excuse herself from all conversation. Why did it affect her so much? Had she been foolish enough to believe that she'd never see Dev with any other woman? Even if she had misunderstood the relationship between him and Aniya, the whole scene had brought a glaring realization upon her.

Dev didn't belong to Rose.

He was open for all woman to look at, have a conversation, touch, kiss or maybe even more.

She shuddered at the thought. Her mind debated the idea of leaving when something warm touched her waist, startling her.

"Easy there." the familiar low baritone cautioned.

She didn't turn, didn't face him.

"Enjoying the races?" Dev inquired casually.

"Absolutely!" she retorted, compensating a lack of eye contact with a louder cheer in her tone. "I'm thinking of placing a bet."

He grew curious. "Really?"

"Yes. I've developed a fondness to that one, number four." She had no idea what she was saying but her tongue seemed to move at it's own accord.

"Number 4, huh?"

"Yes, he was quite good, don't you think?"

"Not particularly." He remarked. "Since, she didn't run in the last race at all."

"Oh... my bad. I think I meant number five. See, that one" she pointed in the general direction of the track, without really pausing to check. The lanes were empty.

Dev frowned.

"Maybe they've left. I might've missed it." The words continued, unrestrained and marvelous in their nonsense. "Now that I'm thinking about it, where do the horses go at the end of the race. Is there a rest area? Do a dozen men huddle around them, like..." she chuckled, nervously, "Formula1."

Someone needed to physically close her mouth at this point.

"Listen." Dev said, delicately as if he were addressing a miffed child. "I think I know what the problem is. Let..."

"Problem?" Rose laughed, distractedly "There's no problem. I'm getting quite hungry. Do you want to get something to eat?"

She moved to turn but his arm wrapped around her waist, pulling her back.

She snapped. Before he could say anything, her elbow thrust into his chest, causing him to groan audibly. "Rose!"

"Let go of me." She whirled to face him. "You cannot simply grab me whenever you please."

"What the hell is wrong with you?" he hissed, recovering from the unexpected blow.

For a second Rose regretted her actions. But the regret lasted only until her eyes fell on his left cheek. Someone else had pressed their lips right there. Rage filled her once again. "Do you go around grabbing other women?" she accused.

Dev, who had by now straightened himself, gave her a stupefied glance. Women had gone crazy today. Someone had randomly kissed him and another had just elbowed him. Already on the edge over his own feelings, he was getting annoyed.

"What," he bit between his teeth, "other women?"

"Oh, of course." She chuckled, darkly. "There are so many options that you require specifics."

"You're angry, I get it." This was about Aniya, he knew. So he tried to reason calmly.

Rose, however, was in her own world of bone shaking envy.

"Oh why should I be angry." she announced, throwing her hands up. "Go grab other women. Why do I care!"

He was getting tired of this 'other women' business. For fuck's sake, there were other women around and he wished he would've been able to notice them. But for some forsaken reason, he was consumed by this ridiculous girl who was driving him crazy. He reached for her, but she nudged him away. This was stupid. She was getting bothered over nothing. He had come here to explain his very platonic relationship with Aniya, and Roman's stupid plan which seemed fit only for silly teenagers.

Dev started, calmly. "That girl you saw, she's...."

"Aniya Malhotra, I know. You don't need to make introductions. I'm not at all interested in meeting you precious friend."

Dev's eyes narrowed with intrigue. He had expected some irritation on her part but not a reaction this strong. He hadn't considered genuine, visible envy.

"You're actually jealous." he observed, incredulously.

"Jealous? I'm not jealous!" Averting his gaze, she crossed both arms over her chest.

Dev hated when Roman's stupid antics actually became of consequence. But Dev had to admit - he had become invested in this new development. Slowly, he took a step toward her. Her arms dropped to the side but she continued to look away.

The crowds cheered as another race commenced. No one noticed them standing in a forgotten corner, far too close to each other.

"My mistake. Why should you be this jealous?" he drawled in a dangerous whisper.

Had she been more rational and in control of herself, she would've realized fairly easily that he was teasing her. But she wasn't in control. She was fuming, her face red with open anger.

"Look at me." he ordered.

"No." she bite, promptly.

Something deep inside him wanted laugh. And something else wanted to kiss her.

"Rose..." he tilted his head sideways.

Blue eyes fluttered to meet his gaze and for a moment he was taken aback from their intensity.

"She kissed you." The accusation was sharp and piercing. "And you let her."

His mouth closed into a thin line neither acknowledging, nor denying.

Despite her best judgment, despite every impulse in her mind screaming not to admit it...not to voice the thought which would only act as an open spark before a flammable mountain, she said the words - "She had no right!"

Her breath was labored now, audible and heavy. He closed the remaining distance between them, very quickly. Her face was just inches below his. If he leaned in, just a little bit, he would've consumed her.

Instead, he breathed, "Then who does?"

The question hit her like physical force. Her mouth parted in shock, eyes wide in wonder as sanity rushed in, forcibly reminding her that his question was a trap that she had willingly walked into.

A trap which for some reason, didn't feel as scary as it did days before.

She stumbled backward, raising one quick hand to stop his arm that had automatically risen to aid her.

The question remained long after she'd whirled around and dashed into the crowd. It remained as he watched her disappear amongst the sea of hats and fascinators. It remained as he stood alone watching the majestic horses gallop; the violent sound of hooves no match for the violent pleasure that coursed through his body. He'd never imagined that he's see her inflamed with jealousy.

His masculine pride roared.

Envy, he concluded with a dark smile that lit a fire in his eyes, looked devastatingly beautiful on her.

Chapter 24

Roman's beach house was built on a piece of land that was bought three generations before him, at a time when it was considered useless. Now, of course, it was worth a small fortune. A large, well-constructed porch at the back of the house opened directly onto the sandy beach, beyond which lay the expanse of the ocean.

It was an experience in itself, to spend an evening in a space that even though was built on land, felt like it was part of the ocean.

Most of guests who attended the racing event were present at the after party. It began late in the evening. People had changed out of their formal attire, opting for more relaxed clothing. The women wore short, daring outfits, their hair loose and free. The men abandoned coats and ties and chose casual pants and loose shirts. Some put on comfortable sandals, others went barefoot altogether.

Stylish outdoor seating had been set up on the section of the beach adjoining the porch. A bonfire lay in the center, emerging from the sand, drawing everyone towards it.

Dev was reclined on one of the wicker chaises surrounded by his usual group - a few cousins and a few close friends. Nash was traveling again and

Dev's own sister was away on one her sporadic escapades with her college friends.

Nia and Aniya were immersed in deep conversation. Aniya said something causing Nia turn to Dev, a nervous expression on her face.

"What?" Dev asked, irritated.

Nia shook her head swirling the drink in her hand instead.

"Where's your..." Aniya said, pausing with deliberate effect, "friend?"

Dev scowled at Aniya.

She chuckled. Throwing her hands up she asked, "I just want to know if my little... skit had any effect?"

"What skit?" Nia interjected.

Aniya responded at once, eagerly recounting the afternoon proceedings.

"You what!" Nia shouted, her eyes wide in shock. "Dev!" she turned toward him. "Is this true?"

Dev who'd had enough women ruining his day, threw her warning look.

Nia wasn't deterred. "You made her think that you and Aniya were a thing!"

"I did no such thing." Dev retorted with irritation. "Roman and Aniya..."

"But you let her believe it." Nia turned to Aniya and admonished, though more politely than she had spoken to Dev, "And you shouldn't have done that."

A visible line of regret ran on Aniya's face. She opened her mouth to explain but before she could, a male voice drifted in from the behind them.

"Sometimes people need a push." Roman drawled, coming to take a seat beside Nia. He put one arm around her shoulder that promptly received a sharp smack. He grinned at her, unperturbed.

Roman and Nia had only met recently since the latter had moved to Vancouver after finishing grad school. They had formed an unlikely friendship that had surprised many, especially when it came to Roman. He had causal dates, flings and exes but not female friends. At one point, Dev had suspected that Roman had a crush on his cousin but he realized fairly quickly that there wasn't anything romantic between them. Whatever fondness Roman felt for Nia was something entirely different, too honest, almost familial.

"That was a bad thing to do, Roman."

"I beg to differ." Roman drawled, grinning. "You're too nice. You won't understand these dynamics from your saintly corner somewhere much higher than the rest of us."

"It's not funny"

"Nia, my sweet...sometimes in order to overcome fear, one has to confront terror."

"What is that suppose to mean?"

"You'll see." Roman turned to Dev. "So..."

"So?" Dev challenged.

"How's the girlfriend?"

"I told you..." Dev gritted. "She's not my girlfriend."

Roman shook his head, wryly. "Not yet, anyway." He whispered sardonically, low enough so only Nia could hear.

"It's not our place, Roman." she warned.

"I'm helping my friend." he countered, defensively.

"By hurting his girlfriend!"

"She's not my girlfriend." Dev interjected, livid by now.

Nia scrunched her face in apology, biting back her words.

"All of you - Stop." Dev ordered, sternly. "Whatever your intentions - good or," he gave Roman a pointed look, "devious. Just stop. She isn't my girlfriend. And she's probably never going to be my girlfriend."

Rose stared at her reflection in the mirror one last time. The Uber was only minutes away. She wasn't going to the take the train today. The last few hours had gone by quickly. She mulled over a whirlpool of thoughts while changing her outfit. Twice.

Tonight called for a perfect dress. There was something she had to do.

Envy shouldn't have taken root in her so ferociously. Not when she had truly believed that Dev was better without her. A castle of cards, no matter how well constructed, is still just a flimsy structure, susceptible to the gentlest breeze. Some beliefs, are just that - a grand castle built with flimsy delusions. A single moment of terror is enough to collapse its foundation into rubble.

She entered through the double doors, completely blind to the grandeur of Roman's house. It could've been a palace or a marshy farm, and she would've walked past through both just the same.

When Dev caught sight of the person who had just stepped down from the porch, he was thunderstruck. The drink in his mouth almost sputtered out.

He couldn't believe what she'd done!

The beat of his heart pounded with feral disbelief. No one else would understand the meaning of her actions. And no else was meant to. It was a silent message for him alone. His gaze landed on her face and he gulped. Her entire demeanor had undergone a drastic change.

'So? What are you going to do about it?' a sixteen-year-old had once boasted with an expression that had grown more defiant ten years later.

Her head was held high, nose tipped forward and jaw clenched tight. It was more than just pride. Fuck, it was downright arrogance. She tore through the crowd, barefoot. Her steps were deliberate, unhurried, like someone who's in control of themselves.

With an effort that was surprising in it's necessity, he got on his feet and walked away. His friends followed his line of sight.

"Something happened..." Nia frowned after Dev had left. They had naturally sensed a mysterious vibe between the pair

"That was the girl?" Aniya asked.

"That," Roman grinned, watching Rose as she made her way to the bar, "is Dev Malhotra's girlfriend. Once again."

Rose took her drink from the bartender and turned to find herself face to face with Dev. This time, despite him being several inches taller, she didn't feel that small. His strangled intake of breath gave her a perverse satisfaction. The feeling however was short lived. Murky brown eyes were narrowed with raw intensity. The longer he looked at her, the quicker her resolve crumbled. In an effort to maintain the upper hand, she turned on her heel. It was better to put distance between them.

"Rose" he called, without raising his voice. She heard him over the loud music and turned her torso sideways. Extracting his phone from his pocket, he aimed it towards her retreating form. Her lips were parted naturally and loose brown strands flew with the breeze, slashing across her face. Without asking, without hesitating, he clicked a picture.

She glared at him and turned to leave.

His arm came around her waist and yanked her back. It wasn't a gentle touch. There was no polite consideration.

There was only entitlement.

He held her like it was his right...a right that she had just proclaimed in front of the entire world. He pressed her deeper into him, the rigid muscles of his chest imprinted her back. His head dipped low, hovering over her collar bone. The short stubble grazed against the softness of her skin. He smirked, when she visibly shivered, relishing the responsiveness of her body.

"Let me go." she murmured, angrily. Tiny sparks burnt throughout her body. "People will notice."

"Isn't that what you intended?"

"Let me go." she repeated, indignantly.

"No." he growled into her ear. His free hand stretched high, phone still clutched between his fingers and pointed towards them, clicking photos at random moments. He turned his face sideways.

"Look at me." There was no softness to his voice. Only a command.

The words dropped deep inside her but she somehow found the resolve to rebel. Biting her lower lip, her gaze remained on the phone, instead. She quivered at the image reflected on the screen; his arm wrapped possessively around her. His fingers tightened, molding her to his chest.

"Now, Rose." he warned.

She could resist no longer. Like always, she succumbed to the sound of his voice and turned to lock her eyes with his.

He snapped photos in quick succession, holding her gaze. This was a moment he wanted to remember forever.

"Dev, please." To her dismay, her words wavered.

He sighed, almost frustrated. The slender curve of her shoulder rose, making her appear fragile. Her skin glowed by the light emanating from the bonfire. And just like that, he succumbed to her as well.

She dashed, throwing herself into frenzy of the party.

Her envy had given him a sense of power. In his conceit, he'd posed a dangerous question. Now, as her eyes kept drifting back to him, she was giving him her answer.

Rose Barnes had the ultimate right to Dev Malhotra. She always did...and she always would. There could be no one else. It was her right forever, not because of some extraordinary reason or a hidden secret. No...

It was her right simply because he had given it to her...a very long time ago.

Dev was standing on his two feet but in his mind she had brought him down on his knees.

Over her simple lavender dress of lace and tulle, with her hair loose and wavy and eyes fiery with emotion, she was wearing his old denim jacket...

Chapter 25

After that brief encounter, Dev showed no reaction. It made Rose angrier. She wanted him unhinged, unnerved and vulnerable, like she had been hours ago. She wanted to wield her power over him. Instead his face now held derision, a kind of untouched arrogance.

Dev wanted to laugh. She was so innocent in her rage, so naive in her defiance. Didn't she understand that she'd rendered him completely powerless? And in stripping him away of his power, she had surrendered herself to him. He stared at her, indecently, feeling a strange pleasure burn through his veins. At some point, he made his way away from the crowd, drifting far in the darkness of the beach. She followed.

He walked languidly. She shuffled angrily, behind.

He stopped and turned around. She halted a foot away from him.

The stood silently, facing each other, as the tides rose. The sand beneath was wet and cold. Soft folds of delicate tulle swept along the muddy brownness, staining its lavender hue.

"I thought you weren't jealous." Dev whispered, a dark smirk curving on his lips.

She glared at him. "I'm not."

"Oh," he exclaimed, mockingly, "so this is just a fashion statement? A decade old faded Levis jacket that was purchased on sale for thirty dollars?"

"Twenty-eight. We had gone shopping together."

The moments were filled with the sounds of the rolling waves. She blinked apprehensively. Her fingers curled possessively over the lapels of her jacket.

"I won't give it back." she said, misinterpreting his silence.

His eyes grew wide in shock, mouth slightly open. If she ever gave it back to him, he'd die inside.

"You can go around flirting with other women but..." her breath hitched.

"But?" he challenged.

"They will never have the right." she replied, unwavering.

All humor had left his face. "Why?"

"I'm telling you, that's why."

"Not good enough."

She glowered at him. "No one has the right to you..."

"Why?"

She was consumed with her own thoughts.

"These women can be beautiful, successful and accomplished and have all the money in the world but they still won't have the right."

"Why?" His eyes were narrowed with intensity.

"They can try but no... no one has the right to you —"

"Why?"

"—not one person out there in this whole world"

"Why, Ro?" His voice had dropped to a murmur.

"Because I love you!"

The winds had picked up the words and carried them across the vastness of the ocean; across the expanse of eight years.

She had shouted the words. Out of anger, frustration, exhaustion and, out of the immovable honesty of her soul. Her breathing grew labored and a visible mist formed in her eyes, the blueness in those orbs rivaling that of the night sky above.

He blinked. He should've leapt ahead, taken her in his arms but he stood rooted to the spot.

"I love you, Devraj. I love you more than I knew I was capable of. I loved you back then even when I didn't understand what love was in the first place. I imagined it meant something dramatic, life altering and extraordinary. It is, yes. But it's also the simplest thing in this world. When I'm with you, I feel perfectly at peace, protected and complete. My own demons are afraid of you - they loose their power in your presence. I don't feel that I've failed or made mistakes. I don't feel that I deserve the bad things. When I'm with you, I feel beautiful and safe. I feel that I'm capable of achieving things that I've dreamed of. You make me so intensely happy that I don't know how I ever lived without you."

He should've moved then. He wanted to. He wanted to consume her. But his body remained frozen, only his eyes blinked slowly. She continued:

"Until this morning, I had somehow convinced myself that I could be friends with you. But when I realized that it meant I would have to see you with someone else, it completely broke me inside. I feel so foolish. How could I ever think I could live with you?" She was crying now. "You can't be with anyone else, Dev. You just can't."

He moved. But she stopped him.

"No!" she raised one frantic hand, retreating, bringing in another foot of distance between them. "You don't understand...I can't live without you. I can't see you with some one else. I want you to love me the way you used to. Only me. Just me. Always me. Whether I deserve it or not. I want to know. Now." Her voice derailed with confusion, uncertainty, desperation and fear. "If you still..."

The waves lashed loudly around them. They stood facing one another and for a long minute it seemed like the night sky had paused just to view the pair who were still grappling to embrace the most profound yet simplest feeling in the world.

"If I still love you?" He inquired, evenly. Turning around, he stood with his hands in his pockets. He was staring at the dark nothingness of the beach.

He murmured the next words so softly, she'd almost imagined them. "That you even have to ask." A sigh left him and he shook his head. "Let's race."

Her eyes widened at the sudden proposition. "Now? Here?"

He titled his head and smiled with amusement. "Why? Are you out of practice?"

She pressed her lips, giving him a meaningful look but came to stand beside him. A cold wave swept below their feet, melting away the sand.

"Dev?" she pronounced, softly.

"Hmm?"

"Where is the finish line?"

They weren't on their field...there was no oak tree.

"There." He pointed one finger to the dark, infinite expanse ahead.

Her fingers closed around the fabric of the dress near the thighs, lifting the hem above her feet. "I'm going to win you know."

He glanced at her, peering into her soul. "I wouldn't have it any other way." He got into a running stance, one foot ahead of the other, "On you mark."

She focused at the non-existent finish line. He focused on her.

"Get set."

She set off!

His face broke into a broad smile. He'd always given her a head start and he would do so for the rest of their lives. Except today, it wasn't just a head start. He was waiting to let the image sink into the depths of his memory.

The image of his Rose, her lush brown hair flying with the wind. Footsteps impressed onto the wet sand as she ran barefoot while a wispy trail of tulle floated in her wake. When she threw him a glance, there was an innocent mirth in her eyes. The moonlight cast an ethereal glow on her lavender dress, his old faded jacket somehow perfectly complimenting it. His heart felt weak and he grew breathless.

It took him barely any effort to catch up. When his arms came around her waist, she gasped, turning her body fluidly into him. He held her, tight and unyielding. She reveled in his strength, burying her face in the crook of his neck, closing her eyes as the scent of cedar wood and forest consumed her senses. He was catching his breath, just as she was, the hot exhales warming them. He drew back and reached to hold her cheek with his hand. The words that followed were raw and simple:

"I tried to forget you, even resent you. I never succeeded. I think my fate was sealed the moment that adorable twelve-year-old girl, in her white dress with red cherries, extended her hand to the nervous twelve-year-old boy. I fell in love with you years ago. But I never fell out of love. You have always been my life's inspiration...my only inspiration. Everything I do, somehow begins with you. You told me the other day that my world is better than yours. You're right. It is. Because you are my world. When I hold you, when I touch you, I feel a different kind of strength running in my veins. Eight years have taught me that there is a difference between breathing and living. I don't want to just breath. I want to live. I love you, Rose. Just you. Only you. Always you. You want me to love you like I used to? How can I? When I love you so much more now. And I think by tomorrow, I would've fallen in love with you a little more."

The tears that fell came out of the explosive happiness of her heart. She clung to him, holding on with urgent desperation. "I love you." she whispered, into his neck. "I love you."

His arms tightened, if that was even possible. He inhaled her scent like a dying man, like someone who had been denying himself for far too long and was finally given the gift of indulgence. He caressed her head and stroked the length of her back. His heart thudded erratically. When he kissed her, time seem to stretch. She sighed into his mouth, her entire body conforming against the length of his. They pulled apart and simply remained for long moments.

"You know," she began, regaining her thoughts from before. "I'm still mad at you."

He pushed a lock of hair to tuck it behind her ear. "Why, sweetheart?"

She blushed. Again. It would take a long time to get used to his endearments. Forcing her voice with more control, she said, "You and Aniya were..."

His laughter rang through the air before she even completed her sentence.

"It's not funny!" She hit his chest, causing him to stumble backward as he continued laughing shamelessly.

"Sweetheart, listen..."

"Don't! You were flirting with her and kissing her. All afternoon."

"I wasn't flirting." he corrected, lofty and smirking. "And I didn't kiss her. She kissed me. On the cheek."

"But you let her!"

He grinned. "There's nothing between Aniya and me. She's an old friend."

"Nothing?"

He shook his head, loving the way evident relief flooded onto her cheeks.

"She's going to be engaged." As an afterthought, he added, "to someone else."

"You ass..." Seething, her small frame leapt to land a punch at him. Then a kick. A shove there. A few more punches. Feeble attempts to mask her wounded heart. While aiming a particularly nasty kick, a heavy wave of water swept underneath, drawing out copious amounts of sand from beneath their feet. She lost her balance and would've fallen had it not been for his solid arm that wound around her waist, nearly lifting her off her feet. She groaned and her fists still attempted to push him away. In a firm motion, he jerked her closer, pressing her chest flush against his, stilling her movements.

"Shhh..." he soothed into her ears. "So beautiful you are... my very own Rose."

His voice resonated from somewhere deep within his chest, vibrating against her palms.

"You let me believe all day that you were into someone else." she whispered, her lips drawn into a wounded pout. Her eyes were lowered, focusing on a spot on his chest. "And you haven't even said sorry."

"I'm sorry." he breathed against the side of her forehead.

She glanced up, slowly, searching his face. "No, you're not."

"You're right." he conceded instantly. "I'm not sorry. How else would I have seen - you stepping onto the beach wearing my jacket?"

Her teeth tugged at her plump lower lip. Dev couldn't help himself. He ran his thumb over the rosy flesh. When she shivered, his own desire surged.

"You kept it." He grew solemn with hints of disbelief. "Why?"

She answered with a quiet conviction. "Because you gave it to me."

The swell of his Adam's apple moved slowly along the length of his neck. There was raw yearning in his eyes. He tugged at the denim collar of her jacket which sat higher than it should. "It still doesn't fit you."

"No, Dev." she looked into his eyes, letting him inside her most vulnerable space. "It's the only one that fits me...perfectly."

He lowered his mouth over hers, kissing her slow and languid.

She moaned evoking a raw masculine sound from his chest. Moments later, she pulled apart, gasping for air. Her eyes drifted to the ongoing festivities far behind them.

"Do you want to go back to the party" she asked, "Your friends must be waiting for you."

"At this point I believe they're waiting to meet you."

Her heart picked up it's pace.

"Or we can just walk to my place."

"Your place?" She looked confused. "Isn't it a half an hour drive?"

He shook his head and looked over her shoulder. Her eyes followed his line of sight to see that they were standing ahead of a different house, very similar to Roman's.

"How many houses do you own!" she groaned, staring at the sprawling mansion in wonder.

He chuckled. "To be fair, that belongs..."

"To your father...yeah I get it." She smiled, dropping her head on his shoulder and looked at the house with wistful resignation. "I can never compete with any of this. But I promise, whatever I do, whatever I achieve...I'll give it to you."

He raised her chin with two fingers. "I don't want anything...just you." Lowering his head, he whispered into her ear. "You're mine now, Ro." Then added, teasingly, "Finally."

She blushed, burying her face into his chest again. "Will you let me win every race?" she asked, the words muffled into the fabric of his shirt.

"Always."

"Even when I run at 'Get set'?

There was a pause. "On one condition."

She tipped her head up to meet his eyes. "What condition?"

He ran one hand along the side of her body and lowered his mouth a breath away from her lips. "You have to promise to run every race with me. Only me."

Her eyes grew misty. "I promise."

The tides grew high and the sand beneath her shifted. But she didn't find herself tipping backward this time. He held her easily, fiercely, eliminating the need for solid ground. She buried herself into his chest, letting him consume her in the warmth of his body. There would be many days to talk, months and years, hopefully. For now, she just wanted to be held by him.

Far away, Roman, Nia, Aniya and a few other closed friends noticed the hazy sight of two figures locked together. They smiled at each other, even cheered silently, and raised a toast. The party went on and ended. The lights dimmed then went away altogether. People left to go back to their lives. But time had stilled for those two people who had found their whole world right there, in that moment, amidst the rolling waves and the starry sky.

The End

www.ingramcontent.com/pod-product-compliance
Lightning Source LLC
Chambersburg PA
CBHW070952180726
48291CB00004B/1263